BLOOD OATH

"ARE YOU READY TO JOURNEY INTO the folds of The Order of Thieves?"

"I am."

Cat picked the chain up from the table. "This chain symbolizes your birth into The Order."

Banit leaned forward so Cat could place the chain around his neck. Then Cat picked up the Bible and held it out. "Place your hand on the Bible and repeat after me. 'With this oath, I swear with my life to uphold The Order. To obey and follow all its rules and to always strive to better the principles it is founded upon and to walk in their deeper meanings.'"

After Banit repeated the oath, Cat placed the Bible down and moved on to the bullet. He picked it up, then moved over to a bowl of ashes and dipped the tip of the bullet in it. Cat put the bullet tip on Banit's forehead, making an imprint with the ashes. "May this bullet strike you dead should you violate The Order."

Next, Cat thrust his hand into the ashes and withdrew a needle between his thumb and forefinger. Cat took hold of Banit by the wrist and turned his hand over, palm up. A glint of light caught the needle's point before Cat plunged it into his friend's pointer finger. Drops of blood trickled off Banit's finger into the bowl. "May your blood turn to ashes should you violate The Order of Thieves."

Both men looked at each other and smiled now that the ritual was complete. Cat then walked around the table and hugged his friend. "Welcome, my brother."

RESPECT THE JUX

FRANK C. MATTHEWS

Pocket Books / Karen Hunter Publishing
NEW YORK LONDON TORONTO SYDNEY NEW DELHI

Pocket Books
A Division of
Simon & Schuster, Inc.
1230 Avenue of the Americas
New York, NY 10020

Karen Hunter Publishing
A Division of
Suitt-Hunter Enterprises, LLC
P.O. Box 692
South Orange, NJ 07079

This book is a work of fiction. Names, characters, places, and incidents either are products of the author's imagination or are used fictitiously. Any resemblance to actual events or locales or persons, living or dead, is entirely coincidental.

First Karen Hunter Publishing/Pocket Books paperback edition September 2012

POCKET and colophon are trademarks of Simon & Schuster, Inc.

For information about special discounts for bulk purchases, please contact Simon & Schuster Special Sales at 1-866-506-1949 or business@simonandschuster.com.

The Simon & Schuster Speakers Bureau can bring authors to your live event. For more information or to book an event contact the Simon & Schuster Speakers Bureau at 1-866-248-3049 or visit our website at www.simonspeakers.com.

Designed by Jamie Lynn Kerner

Manufactured in the United States of America

10 9 8 7 6 5 4 3 2 1

ISBN 978-1-4516-7254-1
ISBN 978-1-4391-9395-2 (ebook)

To all who have fallen victim to the streets; to those who lost their lives; to the mothers who have lost their sons; to all the wives who no longer have their husbands; to all the men who've lost their freedom; to the little girls and boys whose mothers struggle to raise them—without a father; and to all the families and friends who stand by our sides in our time of need.

To the hustlers who maintain and live by the unwritten code; to the nine-to-fivers and all those who have fallen victim to the jux; and to those who have lived it and are able to tell their stories.

To all who respect the jux.

Now repeat after me: "I, with this oath, swear with my life to uphold The Order. To obey and follow all its rules and to always strive to better the principles it is founded upon and to walk in their deeper meanings."

ONE

Banit held his gun up examining it, then took a deep breath, giving Cloud the signal that he was ready for anything. Cloud gently turned the gold door handle. When they stepped into the room, the floorboard made a loud screeching sound. Banit and Cloud froze in their tracks as the couple in the bed began to rouse. A man stumbled out of the bed and started ruffling through the nightstand drawer. The woman came at Banit aggressively, her nails attempting to claw his face. Banit pushed her out of the way, trying to see what the man was looking for in the drawer. Cloud leaped over the bed and landed on top of the man. The two rolled back and forth across the room trying to get the upper hand. Cloud came out ahead. Banit threw him some rope and he tied up the man. Banit, like the professional that he is, tackled the woman and tied her up in no time. The woman sat in the corner, next to her man, with tears streaming down her face.

Then three shots rang out from Banit's gun.

Cloud, with reflexes like that of a striking black mamba, spun around and dropped to his knees, aiming his pistol in the direction from which he'd heard the shots. Prince, who was also downstairs conducting his own search, quickly drew his gun and methodically shifted out of another room and made his way down the hall to investigate the gunfire. He stopped about three feet from the living room's entrance.

"Yush!" he called out in his Jamaican accent. It was a code that only his men knew the meaning of.

"It safe," Banit replied.

Ozzi, who is extremely paranoid, was searching the basement when he heard the shots. He didn't believe in taking chances. Gun in hand, he crept through the door of the living room. He saw Prince. Prince waved to him, assuring Ozzi that it was all clear. They both were still on edge.

Banit and Cloud were standing over a bullet-riddled corpse.

"What the fuck just happened?" asked Ozzi.

"The man have a tool on him ankle," said

Banit, referring to the gun the dead man had hidden in his sock. "Somehow him loosen him hand and reach for it. Me see him just in time before him lick off Cloud head."

"Well, you know the deal," Ozzi said. "Works is blown, time to clean and backtrack fast."

Ozzi directed everyone to get the hell out of there. Their mission would have to be left incomplete.

"What about her?" asked Cloud, pointing to the young lady bound and gagged next to the man's lifeless body.

"She knows what we look like, so we have to dust her," said Banit, trying to be the voice of reason. "She heard us talking; she can distinguish us as yardy."

"We have to dust her," Ozzi agreed.

The young lady's eyes were now wide-open. Death's rancid scent was in the air. Her muffled cries didn't deter the four men from gathering around her with their guns drawn. She lay there helplessly, pleading with her eyes. Ozzi fired the first shot into her chest. Then he pointed his gun at Banit, who fired a shot in the same spot. Then both of them pointed their guns at Prince, who fired into her lifeless body as well. All three men pointed their guns at Cloud, who hesitated at first, but eventually fired the last round.

Each man had to fire a round into the body to ensure that each of them incurred responsibility for her murder. If one of them refused to do so, he would immediately be shot dead by the remaining men per a code of The Order. These cold-blooded killers lived by these codes.

The crew returned to The Lodge, in a cul-de-sac in a quiet, middle-class section of Queens. Its earth-tone painted colors gave it somewhat of a low profile. Like most houses in the neighborhood, it was concealed by a six-foot privacy fence. Large maple trees stood in the yard, casting dark shadows like that of a mystic giant. In the windows hung thick cotton curtains that prevented light from entering or exiting.

"You didn't search him when you tied him up?" shouted Ozzi as soon as the door closed.

"Yes," answered Cloud.

"So where'd the gun on his ankle come from, Magic?" Banit asked.

"I guess me just missed it," replied Cloud.

"What? You guess you just missed it?" Ozzi echoed in a sarcastic tone. "You caused a potentially good jux to be blown. Any of us could have gotten killed because you guess you just missed it." He made mocking quotation marks with his fingers.

"We don't have no big 'I' or little 'you' here," Ozzi continued. "But something has to be done to show you how serious you fucked up. Hear this—the next jux we come off with, seventy-five percent of your share gets split up between the three of us."

Every man in the room was a gunman, which by their definition was not the same as a gangster. In Jamaica, a gangster would use the police in certain instances, but a gunman would have absolutely no dealings with the police. He handled business on his own.

In fact, whenever a gunman and a cop come face-to-face, you can be sure that a gunfight will erupt. Police in Jamaica do not arrest gunmen, they kill them. Knowing this, a gunman will take his chances in a shoot-out.

Cloud knew he couldn't just walk away from The Order. He knew too much about them, and walking away could cost him his life. He agreed with their terms. Three-quarters of his cut on the next jux would go to the other three members, and that was that.

TWO

Cat founded The Order sometime in the nineties after he was discharged from the U.S. armed forces. He arrived in the United States when he was just sixteen years old. His mother had already been living in the States and wanted Cat and his sister to emigrate from Jamaica—to get away from certain elements and have a chance at a better life. Little did she know, by the time she sent for him, Cat was already a full-blown crook.

Cat's father was a high-ranking member of a gang in Kingston, Jamaica. He was murdered by a rival gang member when Cat was seven. After the death of his father, his mother traveled to the States in quest of a better life. She was unable to take Cat and his sister along since she was traveling on a visiting visa. She left Cat and his sister in the hands of their aunt, who lived in a Kingston ghetto.

Cat was forced to grow up quickly. His mother sent money back home every month, but it was hardly enough to support the family. Cat started hustling. He was tired of going to bed every night without dinner. He was tired of wearing the same pair of jeans every day. He was tired of not having. By the age of eight, Cat was already snatching purses, shoplifting, and climbing through open windows.

A neighborhood general named Stark had been keeping an eye on Cat for a while. He noticed how crafty the young Cat was. Stark also noticed the hunger, the drive to make it. The general gave Cat his first gun—a .38 Special. Getting a gun was tough in Jamaica. Guns were sacred and, thus, worshipped.

The gun was so old and rusted that it wasn't operational. The firing pin was worn-out and the trigger was seized up. Nevertheless, it would make for a good scare.

This was the gun all the new recruits started with. They would be sent out on a jux, and if they were successful, the money would be given to the don, who gave a kickback to the generals, and the generals would give their new recruits whatever they decided. When Cat was ten, he committed his first robbery with a gun.

This was their system. You had to work your way from the bottom up, and the danger was that all the young recruits aspired to be a don someday.

Most of the murders were carried out by kids and teenagers—recruits. After a killing, the perpetrator would be sent into hiding. Once things cooled down, he would emerge with stripes and a better position. This would lead to better food and clothing.

Cat was fifteen when he committed his first murder. The owner of a gas station was being stubborn, deciding he wasn't going to pay the local don any protection fees. He felt quite capable of handling his own security and got himself a licensed gun that he kept on his waist at all times.

Cat was given a working gun along with the orders to kill the man, take his weapon, and rob the gas station. On a bright sunny day, Cat walked past the gas pumps and into the store. It was empty except for the owner. Cat didn't raise any eyebrows. He was just your average-looking, malnourished neighborhood kid. He sported a nappy Afro atop his tall, skinny frame. He asked for a pack of cigarettes and a pack of gum.

After he paid for both items, he turned and walked out of the store. That was his test run. Cat was a smart kid. He wasn't about to do anything stupid. He had to feel the guy out first. The following day he returned, this time a little later in the afternoon. He asked for a pack of cigarettes and a soda. He paid, took a quick glance around, and walked out.

Cat came back again two days later. This time the old man recognized him, and before Cat could say anything, he had already turned to get a pack of cigarettes from the shelf behind him. "Cigarettes, right?"

"Yes, and a soda," Cat responded.

"Right, I forgot the soda," the man said cheerfully as he grabbed a can nearby and placed it atop the counter next to the cigarettes. "Anything else?"

Cat scanned the shelf behind the old man and intentionally appeared to be indecisive. The old man watched his eyes wander.

"Yes, let me get one of those grape bubble gums, please."

"Coming right up," the old man said, turning and reaching up for the gum.

Immediately, Cat reached into his waist to grab his gun and aimed it at the old man's back. When the old man turned around, he was staring down the barrel of a hatchback .32 caliber. Cat had never before fired a gun. His arm was shaking and sweat was pouring down his temples.

The general's voice rang in his head: "Just squeeze di trigga."

Cat's hands began to shake. The old man was silent and his glassy eyes were haunting. But Cat feared the general's wrath more. He had no choice. It was either kill or be killed. He shut his eyes tight and squeezed the trigger.

His eyes widened from the booming blast, the recoil of the gun in his hand. The old man fell backward from the impact, clutching his chest as he hit the shelves behind him. As he collapsed, he whimpered.

Cat was afraid. His first impulse was to run. But he stood there frozen, as if the man's blood, which was now flowing freely, was cementing his feet to the floor. His eyes bulged from their sockets as he watched the man's body slide down the shelves toward the floor. Cat's chest heaved up and down as if he had run a mile due to the release of adrenaline into his bloodstream. Cat's hands began to shake as he realized that he might have to fire another bullet into the wounded man. He stepped closer to the counter to better watch his victim.

"Wat the blood claat?" he uttered as he looked down at the bleeding man on the floor, who was in critical condition but far from dead.

The old man managed to reach into his waistband for his gun, releasing the safety. He struggled, slowly raising the gun in Cat's direction. As the storekeeper pointed his gun at Cat's abdomen and prepared to pull the trigger, Cat came to life and pumped three more rounds into the man's chest, killing him instantly. Cat turned quickly to look out onto the streets to see if anyone was in sight. When he was assured that there was no one, he turned and approached the counter.

"Make sure you don't get caught and be sure to get his gun!" General Stark had drilled into Cat's head. He grabbed the cash, the storekeeper's gun, and anything else he could grab for himself. Then he walked out as if nothing had happened. He seemed cool on the outside, but inside, he knew he never wanted to kill another human being again. He could feel the pain in the storekeeper's eyes, and then the peace when life left him. Two emotions, so gravely opposing that when they abrasively collided, they burned through Cat upon impact. He did not want to experience that again.

To Jamaica's criminal underworld, Cat had officially become a man on this day, but in actuality, he had become a cold-blooded killer. The trauma of his first murder and the bloody images would stay with him forever. For the next three months, Cat went into hiding.

He stayed in a village on the island, in a

section called the country. There he lived with his grandmother in a hut, which had no running water or indoor toilet. He had to fetch water from the well or the local stream and use an outhouse. There was no such thing as a telephone, and the closest store was eleven miles away, which he and his grandmother traveled to on foot. Most of the people in the village had never been to the city or owned a television or ridden in a car. Cat wasn't used to living in such a manner and found it difficult to adjust. Life with his grandmother in the village was a hardship. He spent most of his time sitting around thinking of the city and longing to return to his way of life.

When he reemerged, he was feared throughout the neighborhood. He gained even more stature than he could have imagined. While Cat was gone from the street scene, killings continued. Unbeknownst to him, he was being credited for the murders. The rumors stated that the don had Cat hidden outside the city limits and would sneak him back and forth to commit murder. Eight murders were attributed to Cat. He was a subject of discussion every day. Even the authorities were afraid of him. They made it a point to talk with the local don and make a deal. They bargained that if the killings stopped, they would not arrest Cat or any of the other members of the don's gang. Cat was sent word that it was okay for him to return to the city.

Three months later, after Cat's return to Kingston, his aunt called him and his sister into the kitchen, where she sat in a chair at the table holding some papers in her hand.

"Both of you sit down," she told them, pointing to the chairs opposite her.

Cat and his sister did as they were told.

Cat had begun to worry that something was wrong with his mother. "What's going on?"

"Well, I have some good news and some bad news for the two of you. Okay, I'll start with the good news first. The two of you are going to the States to join your mother."

Cat's sister jumped up excited with her arms outstretched. "Oh my God, Auntie, are you serious? We're going to America?"

Cat sat emotionless.

"Yes, the two of you are going to America."

"So, if that's the good news, what's the bad news?" Cat demanded.

"The bad news is that I'm going to miss the two of you," their aunt said, looking at them as her eyes instantly swelled with tears.

Two weeks later Cat and his sister's tickets were purchased by their aunt with money sent to her by their mother. They were on their way to America the following day.

Upon their arrival, their mother picked them up at John F. Kennedy Airport. She took them to their new home, an apartment complex in a middle-class section of Queens, called Rego Park.

There, Cat and his sister were enrolled in school. Because of his age, he was placed in the tenth grade. He was a great student, maintaining a B average and getting an A in one or two classes every term. Being the new kid, he pretty much kept to himself. Though other Jamaicans attended the school, he avoided hanging out with them too much on the advice and pleas of his mother. All that she required of him was that he go to school and get good grades. This was easy for him to do because he was smart and able to accomplish just about anything he put his mind to doing.

He did have one vice—his lust for money and material things. He envied those students with the designer clothes and expensive sneakers. He liked the diamond-encrusted jewelry that he saw the other kids wearing and promised himself to get some as soon as he could afford it. Cat also noted that those who had the money, clothes, and jewels also had the prettiest girls in the school. He wanted a pretty girl, too. Cat recognized at an early age that girls like men with money.

His mother begged him to attend college after he graduated, but instead he enlisted in the army. Cat spent the next four years in the military, going through combat and weapons training. He also completed an engineering program, an area of study that fascinated him. He was well trained and disciplined, knowing how to take orders, as well as give them when stepping into a leadership role. Fortunately, he was discharged right before his unit was called to serve in the Iraq War.

Armed with his military training and engineering education, Cat figured that he would easily take the world by storm. However, he returned to civilian life when the job market was poor and the economy was failing. He searched for a job within his field of expertise, but was not hired.

The best job he could find was working at a nearby supermarket. He did a variety of jobs—unpacking boxes, stocking shelves, sweeping and mopping the store at night after closing—making enough to get by on, but not enough to survive. This wasn't the life he dreamed he would have in America. His vision of America was one of wealth and easy living. Cat always heard stories in Jamaica that a good and easy life was to be found in the States for everyone living there. Making money was supposed to be easy, and if someone was poor, the government would send that person money monthly. He was always told that if he went to school and got an education, he would be able to get a great job and live a good life. The American dream to him was having a nice home, a fancy car, fine clothes, a pretty woman, and money in the bank. Needless to say, he had none of that. Instead, he found himself standing in a supermarket with a broom and a mop in his hands. It was an insult to his integrity.

He wondered how high he would have risen in rank had he stayed in Jamaica. He gave serious thought to going back and even becoming a don, although he knew he'd have to murder more people to reach that status. Truthfully, at the end of each day he knew it was all just wishful thinking because no matter how hard things might get here in the States, he was still better off. At least he didn't have to worry about being broke and hungry or constantly wonder where his next meal would come from or even if the next kid who he assumed was a friend would put a bullet in his head to earn some stripes.

THREE

Cat moved about in the store doing odd things to stay busy. He watched the customers as they came, shopped, and left. Every now and then he would approach a female and try to talk to her. At times, he would get the girl's number, but he was usually rejected. Cat felt that this was because of his low-level job at the store. When he wasn't trying to pick up girls, he would stand at the front of the store, as it allowed him to get a look at everyone, especially Wendy, a checkout girl he liked. He had been trying to win her over for weeks.

While Cat was straightening out the shopping carts from the express line at the supermarket, he noticed a young baller. All the gold rings on the baller's fingers and the two thick gold chains around his neck caught Cat's eye. Cat watched the twentysomething in admiration as he made his way toward the cash register. Cat's eyes widened when the young man pulled out a large, folded knot of cash. He must have been holding at least $1,000. Cat had never held that much money in his hands before. Cat looked on as the stranger peeled off a twenty and handed it to Wendy, who was smiling and blushing. The young moneyman paid for his sodas, insisting Wendy keep the change.

"Gold-diggin' bitch," Cat said under his breath. For months he had been trying to hook up with Wendy, but she wouldn't give him the time of day. Now here came someone flashing his cash and jewelry and she could hardly contain herself.

The moneyman made his way out to the parking lot. Inconspicuously, pushing a chain of carts, Cat followed. He saw the kid approach a Mercedes-Benz. Quickly, Cat ran to the VW he drove to and from work, which belonged to his mother. Cat was captivated by the young moneyman. He wanted to shine like him and impress all the girls. Most of all, he wanted to leave behind his mundane life that seemed to be going nowhere.

As the Benz pulled out of the parking lot and stopped at a red light, Cat was four cars behind. His sweaty palms gripped the steering wheel tightly as he trailed the Benz onto the highway. Two exits later, they got off and traveled on the main strip. After passing several stoplights, the Benz turned off onto a less busy road. Cat had to fall back now because at times there were no cars between them. To avoid being spotted he had to allow the Benz to move ahead, then race to each corner to catch up whenever the vehicle made a turn. Inevitably, Cat didn't make it to one corner in time to see which direction the Benz had turned.

"Bloodclaat," he shouted, realizing he was late in the chase. He raced out to the next corner and pulled out into the intersection so he could look both ways up the street. "Fuck, fuck, fuck," he shouted, banging his fists on the steering wheel. "Left, right, left, right, come on . . . which way did you go, motherfucka?"

Cat raced to the next corner and pulled out into the intersection, again looking in both directions. There was still no sign of the car. He had clearly lost the Benz. Cat pounded away at the steering wheel until it occurred to him that the driver of the Benz might purposely be trying to lose him. But just as abruptly as the thought entered his mind, he dismissed it.

Cat spent the next few hours driving around the neighborhood looking into driveways for the car, but to no avail. Then he suddenly remembered he was still on the clock back at his job. "Shit!" was all he could say as he realized he might not have a job to get back to. He drove around for another half hour before finally calling it quits.

The very next day, Cat pulled off the highway at around the same time of day where he had lost track of the Benz. Car after car passed, but no black Benz. He sat at that same spot looking at cars for the next four days straight. Cat decided to give it up. He turned the key in the ignition and drove off thinking how foolish he was for walking off his job. He made a left turn to get back onto the highway, trying to figure out a way to get his job back. *What kind of crazy story could I tell my boss?*

He flicked the radio on as "My Way" by Usher was playing. He was merging with the highway traffic when he suddenly could not believe his eyes. There it was—the black Benz was two cars ahead of him. Cat pulled up to the Benz's rear bumper to definitely make sure that it was him. Cat was determined not to lose him this time. That's when a thought hit him: *The nigga definitely gotta live somewhere in this neighborhood.*

Cat followed the Benz closely off the highway into a Brooklyn neighborhood that was not familiar to him, Bergen Beach, a conservative and ethnically diverse area. Cat had lived in various sections of Queens his entire time in the United States. Rarely did he have a reason to go to Brooklyn for anything.

Moneyman pulled into the driveway of a brownstone. From his rearview, Cat watched the guy knock on the door, but could not see who let him inside. Cat waited for a short while. He got back on the highway and headed back to the neighborhood where he figured the kid lived. It was a huge risk, but he estimated it was worth it. This time, he'd have to jump on him. Cat pulled up at the same corner where he'd lost Moneyman days earlier, hoping he'd drive back this way.

Three hours later, there was the Benz. Cat started his car and got ready to follow him. But before he could shift the car into drive, Cat noticed the brake lights of the Benz come on. Cat ducked his head a bit, then noticed the car was pulling into a driveway right in front of him. *Fuck outta here, the bitch-ass nigga lived here all this time and I'm drivin' around like a fool lookin' for him.* He watched as Moneyman exited the car and entered the house. Cat drove home.

At around 3 a.m., Cat returned. This time, he didn't pull up on the same block as the house. Instead, he parked a block over, behind a different house, and under a tree. Dressed in all black with gloves and a mask, he turned the ignition off and sat listening to his own breath for a while. *Just this one time. This guy obviously doesn't need the money. Just this one time to get enough money to rest on while I look for a legit job. Just this one time . . .*

He looked around at the surrounding homes to see if any nosy neighbors were peeping out their windows. The coast was clear. He climbed over into the passenger seat, opened the door, and stepped out under the darkness and the cover of the trees. He softly shut the passenger-side door and looked around again, making sure no one's eyes were on him. Satisfied, he made his way up the driveway of the house and continued toward the rear, climbing up and over a fence. As his feet touched the ground on the other side, he crouched low, scanning the area. The black Benz was in direct view. Cat utilized his army training, bending at the waist and dropping low as he moved along the bushes until he reached the back windows. He crab-walked his way to another window so he could get a better view inside. There was no sign of movement within the house. It was now or never. Having run through similar scenarios during his army missions, he knew exactly what to bring along with him. Inside his "thief pouch" at his waist were wire cutters, an interchangeable flathead screwdriver, duct tape, small pliers, and an eight-inch-blade knife. Tucked on the right side of his waistband was a P7 pistol, loaded with Parabellum rounds that he'd stolen during his tour.

Cat located the point of entry, a basement window just wide enough for him to slip through. The window had three glass sections, which could be opened and shut by winding the crank on the inside. It was a simple task with a screwdriver. Slowly and gently, Cat separated each sheet of glass from the window frame. He placed each frame, one by one, on the ground, leaning them against the house. Cat took his time, careful not to crack one of the glass partitions, which would cause unwanted noise.

When the third and final piece was removed, Cat placed it along the wall with the other two. As he did so, he caught a quick glimpse of his reflection in the glass. He didn't recognize himself. He did a double take. He slowly brought the glass to eye level again. It was definitely him. His clenched teeth distorted his face, making him look sinister. Was it a sign that he was losing it? Was this whom he wanted to be? He looked up at the night sky and saw nothing but blackness. A cool wind blew and leaves scattered all around him. The sound of the leaves scraping against each other brought him back to reality. He had to go through with the job.

Along the wall, he located the phone line. He used the wire cutter to disable it. Since the neighbors' lines were linked together, he cut their lines as well. He again glanced around to see if his actions were attracting any attention. He crawled through the basement window, landing inside a tiny bathroom. Instinctively he reached for his gun, waiting for his eyes to adjust to the dimness of the house. Silently, he crept through the basement until he reached the stairwell. His heart was thumping loudly. Cool beads of sweat rolled down his back as his body angled up the steps.

His mind began to run wild. *Could he be waiting for me upstairs with his finger on the trigger? Do I really have to go through with this craziness? Should I just let the kid slide? I could just get another job, stay legit, and be okay. I am in America now. Why do this?* He knew it was wrong. Dollar signs floated into his head. He wanted to reach out and grab them all. He shut his eyes tight to take a minute to regain his composure. *You made it this far, and for what? To turn your back now on what could be waiting upstairs? Hell no! This nigga gonna go down*, he said to himself.

More determined, he peered into the living room. Nothing but darkness. With the gun at his right side, he headed across the living room with the left side of his body leading the way. He reached another set of stairs. They squeaked under his weight. "Damn old houses," he muttered under his breath.

He quickly made his way to the top of the steps. On the left was a bathroom. He passed two empty bedrooms before he came to a closed door at the end of the hall. Cat knelt down by the door with his gun in one hand, turning the knob slowly with the other. He pushed it wide-open. In the darkness, he saw the outline of a bed in the center of the room and quickly crept toward it, gun trained on his target. Two figures lay beneath the sheets. His movements did not disturb their sleep. Cat located the light switch, then made his way to the window and shut the curtains. He flicked on the lights. Simultaneously, he yanked the top sheet off the bed and there was young Moneyman and his girl.

The couple was startled by the sudden bright light and the cold burst of air from the sheet being abruptly removed. When they opened their eyes, Cat pointed the gun directly at them. The girl looked to be about twenty or twenty-one years old. Her mouth opened wide as if she was about to scream. Cat quickly silenced her, placing the cold steel of the gun against her skull.

"Shut the fuck up, bitch, if you wanna live. You understand me?"

"Yes," she answered nervously.

"Good, and you understand that?" Cat said, pointing his gun at the young man.

Moneyman nodded his head.

"We should have no problems then. Keep it this way and this bad dream will be over soon. Now move those pillows." Cat wanted to make sure no guns were hidden underneath them. "Now turn over and lay facedown."

Cat pulled out the duct tape and secured both their hands and feet, feeling a sense of control he had not enjoyed since he left the military. Cat turned Moneyman over onto his back and pulled down his pajama bottoms and boxer shorts. Cat reached into his pouch for his pliers and latched them around Moneyman's penis. "That's a pretty fine bitch you have there. It would be a shame not using this anymore to fuck her. So here's the deal. I'm gonna ask you some very simple questions that require very simple answers. Are you ready?"

Moneyman nodded.

"You're doing good for yourself," Cat said sarcastically. "Now, where's the money and the jewelry?"

Moneyman stammered in fear, "B-b-b-bottom drawer of that d-d-d-dresser. The jewelry is in that box on top the d-d-dresser."

Cat had to laugh out loud, he couldn't help himself, "Haa-ha-ha. You stutterin' motherfucka, I'll bust a cap in you ass right now. Ha! Aight, one more question. What will I find at that crib in Brooklyn you went to, and who stays there?"

"I gots t-twelve keys of coke in there."

"Where in the house will I find them?"

"Under the couch in the living room."

"And who did you say stays there?"

"I didn't say. B-b-but no one stays there. Just my stash house."

Cat smiled. Just that simple. Moneyman was a punk after all.

Cat placed the pliers back in his pouch and walked over to the dresser. He opened the bottom drawer and discovered stacks of hundreds, fifties, and twenty-dollar bills. He froze for a second to catch his breath. Never in his life had he seen so much cash. Cat felt a surge of power that he had never before felt, as though he ruled the world. He grabbed the pillows, yanked off their coverings, and threw the pillows across the room. He piled the money inside one pillowcase. When it was full, he filled another. Finally, he threw in the jewelry.

Transferring the jewelry, Cat spotted a gold Rolex watch. He placed it on his wrist, admiring its bling. He then noticed the girl, still on the bed, staring directly at him. She looked sensual with her hands and feet taped up. Her nightgown came just below her butt cheeks, revealing a perfectly round and plump bottom. Her blue panties showed just a little bit. Her complexion was a smooth caramel. Cat smiled. *I know this little-dick Yankee boy ain't slinging the right cockie on this gal.*

Cat tied up the pillowcases and got ready to leave. He asked Moneyman for the keys to the stash house and his Benz. Cat found them on the night table, pocketed them, and went back to untie Moneyman. Cat cut the duct tape from the young man's ankles so he could walk and led him down to the hallway and into one of the empty bedrooms. He reapplied the duct tape. He pulled the phone wire from the wall and used it to further restrain his victim. He hog-tied Moneyman to the radiator.

"Sure is a fine-ass bitch you got. Listen up, yo. If I go to that house and don't find what you say is in there or if I find more than what you say is in there, then I'll know you lied to me and I'm coming back to find out why."

"Nah, man." Moneyman tried to sound calm. "I'm telling you the truth. Everything I told you was the truth."

"It better be. I would really hate to have to return here just to body you and your bitch."

"Be easy, man, I won't try to play you like that. Do I look like I'm trying to die?" Moneyman seemed about to have a panic attack.

Cat smiled at how well the situation was turning out. He was actually surprised at how intimidating he was. "You got a way with you. Smarter than I thought," Cat told him.

"Man, I'm just trying to live. You already got the dough. It ain't nothin' to die for. You know what, playboy? I dig your style. Too bad we had to meet like this. But I can dig it, man, all part of the hustle, comes wit the territory. By the way, if you don't mind me asking, how did you find me?"

Cat crouched down beside the man. Through his mask, he looked Moneyman right in his eyes. "Nigga, you was way too flashy." Cat then bashed Moneyman on the side of his head with the butt of the gun. The kid was knocked out cold.

The girl was alone on the bed in the first bedroom. She was turned on her stomach. She lifted her head and strained her neck to see behind her, where Cat was. *What a gorgeous view,* Cat thought. He walked over to the bed and could feel his dick rising. That girl looked helpless. Cat took hold of her nightgown and slowly raised it above her ass cheeks, fully exposing her blue silk panties. He rested his left palm on her ass and began to massage her cheeks. The girl began to shake her head violently. Cat took out his knife and cut the duct tape that held her ankles together. Tears started to stream down her face. He spread her legs apart while leaning forward to get a better view. He ran his fingers up the length of her inner thighs, massaging the area between her legs. He felt her tensing up. His fingers began rubbing her even harder and she wailed. Cat stopped.

"If your man wasn't such a motherfucker, I would damn sure let you have it," he exclaimed. Cat walked over to the pillowcases on the floor, picked them up, and began to exit.

"Nigga, you ain't shit! You need to take from other niggas 'cause you ain't got no hustle."

Cat turned around in disbelief. Both pillowcases in hand, he walked over to her side of the bed. "What you just said to me?"

She raised her head slightly and gave Cat the I-don't-care-if-you-kill-me look. "You heard me, you ain't shit. He will catch up to your ass and do what he got to do, motherfucker."

"Is that so?"

"Yes, that's so."

Cat turned her over onto her back. She was beautiful. He pulled his knife out again to release her duct-taped wrists.

"What you about to do? Leave it on."

"Shut the fuck up, bitch!"

"I don't have to do a motherfucking thing."

"This bitch is crazy," he said as if talking to himself.

"I'm not scared of you, so you can stop with all that tough Tony shit. Just leave, you got what you came here for."

"You talk too much, bitch. You know what? I got something for you." Cat unzipped his pants, pulled them down along with his boxers to his ankles. Her eyes widened at the sight of his massive cock. She looked on in fright.

"Damn, it looks like a baby's leg, right?" he said sarcastically.

"Don't touch me!"

"I'm going to put something in your mouth to shut you the fuck up."

"Please, I'm sorry. I'll shut up, just don't do this to me."

"It's too late for all that now, bitch." He grabbed her by the head and begin to force her face toward his erected dick. "Open your mouth and suck it, bitch!"

She struggled to push her head back from him to no avail. Cat slapped her viciously and grabbed a handful of her hair. She began to cry. "Let me see you act tough now, bitch. You still wanna act like you tough?"

She moved her head from left to right again and again.

"I guess that means no!" he shouted. "Well, let's see how you like this." He got on the bed and straddled her. With his left hand, he grabbed her throat, and with his right, he grabbed her face, squeezing her cheeks together. She winced in pain. "Open your mouth, bitch." He eased his body up to her chest and tilted her head forward. "You see, I could do whatever I want to do with you. I'm the one in control. So next time you decide to run your mouth to someone, you make sure that you're in the position to defend yourself. You understand me, bitch?"

"Yes, I understand you."

"That's right, now you see things my way."

She gagged as he choked her a little harder.

"What's the matter, you can't breathe, ho?" He released her and got off the bed. He pulled up his underwear and pants, zipped his pants, and buckled his belt. "Well, sweetheart, I have to be leaving now. Just remember what I told your dumb ass.

"I hope you have some aspirins here because you're going to have one hell of a headache when you wake up." Cat then bashed her over the head with the gun, knocking her unconscious. He picked up the pillowcases, placed them over his right shoulder. With a smile on his face, he walked out, closing the door behind him.

Cat went to Moneyman's house in Brooklyn and found the cocaine under the couch just as instructed. He took everything back to his mother's house and locked himself in his room. When he emerged two days later, bag in hand, he knocked on his mother's door.

"Come in."

He pushed open the door and entered. She was lying on her bed watching TV.

"Hi, Mommy."

"What you been up to, boy? I see that your car been parked for the last couple of days. What is it? You done quit your job?"

Cat walked over to his mom's bed and sat the bag on it. "Mom, ask me no questions and I will tell you no lies." He turned the bag upside down onto her bed and emptied its contents. "I want you to buy us a nice house."

His mother slapped her cheeks with both hands, stunned to see so much money. She looked her son in the eye as if she were about to ask him where all the money had come from, but no words passed her lips.

Cat smiled at his mother affectionately, then turned and walked away.

"Cat, please be careful out there."

His mother's words trailed behind him weakly as he left the room. His family was most important to him. He was the man of the family, so he did what he had to do. In yard culture it was not a woman's place to question the actions of a man—son, brother, father, or husband.

Cat was fully aware that Jamaicans were hardworking people. The majority of them were law-abiding, raised their families, and prided themselves on doing the right thing. They valued family and stayed closely knit. Coming to America was an opportunity to make something positive of themselves and help their family members who were unable to obtain a visa to the United States. Doing the right thing also meant not risking the chance of being deported and blowing a chance that so many of their countrymen wished they had. Most of the Jamaicans would work hard, save their money, and invest in real estate to have property and sometimes secondary income with rental units. It was partly Cat's dream, but working at a supermarket was not going to get him there.

FOUR

Cat spent the next couple of weeks trying to get his job back at the supermarket, but the manager refused. Cat also tried to find a better job by looking in the newspaper and sending out hundreds of résumés. No one called him about a job; he did not even get called in for interviews. As a last resort, he contemplated going to college as his mother had always wanted him to do. All the while, in the back of his mind he kept remembering the thrill of robbing Moneyman. How in control he felt. He was the boss and to some degree a dictator of his destiny. Not waiting to see what life had to offer, but going after what he wanted, seemed more appealing with each résumé going out and nothing coming back in.

Cat was no great intellectual, but he was a

visionary. He knew that to pull off a major jux, he'd need some help. Instead of looking for ways to live a legitimate life, he decided to form a secret society of thieves that would simply be called The Order. Cat determined that he would take in no more than six handpicked initiates at a time.

Banit was the first to be inducted into The Order. Banit may have been a lighthearted fellow, but those that weren't familiar with him would surely cross the street if they saw him approaching. He was large, not exactly fat or chubby, but muscular and beefy with broad shoulders, powerful arms, a massive chest, and enormous hands. He was surprisingly agile and athletic for his size. His complexion was dark, and his eyes were even darker. The mere sight of him would strike fear in any man's heart.

After Cat's first robbery, with the advice of his sister, Cat's mother took some of the money and purchased a building as an investment, giving her family something to fall back on. She hired Banit to work as a janitor in the small, rundown two-story building with seven rental units.

Cat lived in the building on the second floor, occupying the largest apartment. It was the only one with a balcony and access to the roof, where he built a deck. He spent most of his time here when he was not out partying or mingling with potential targets. The apartment had two bedrooms and was completely furnished with the latest in everything. He even had a maid that came by twice a week to freshen up the place.

Cat and Banit hit it off well because they were both Jamaican and came from the same background, which eliminated all the hassle of trying to figure out if this person was right for the job. They partied together and Cat paid close attention to every move his friend made. He observed his behavior with the ladies, and the way he spent his money. Cat was particularly watching to see if Banit became careless with his drinking and his tongue. On occasion, Cat would leave Banit alone in his apartment to see if he would go through his things. Banit passed every test with flying colors and proved himself trustworthy.

Cat sat Banit down one day in the living room. He broke down everything about The Order. He told him what he did for a living and that he wanted to initiate Banit as the first inductee in The Order of Thieves. Immediately, Banit saw Cat in a new light. Things began to add up concerning Cat's fancy lifestyle and no obvious job.

That night, Cat drove Banit to a large farm-style house in Bayside, Queens. The house was bought by Cat in his sister's name. It was a quiet and dark neighborhood by the bay, which made it easy to slip in and out without being seen. They pulled into the driveway, exited the car, walked up to the front door, and Cat took out a set of keys. The house had three entrances—front, side door, and back. Cat looked at Banit once more in approval before opening the front door. They walked down a long hallway at least fifteen feet before reaching an altar. Cat asked Banit to read the inscription on the front side aloud.

"'Beside Christ, there were two thieves, the repentant and the impenitent thief,'" Banit recited.

"Don't ever forget that," Cat told him.

They walked past the altar and came to a small table that had a gold chain with a tree-of-life pendant on it. Next to the chain was a Bible and .45-caliber bullet. The last item on the table was a crystal bowl filled with ashes.

Cat walked around to the other side of the table facing Banit and with a serious look asked, "Are you ready to journey into the folds of The Order of Thieves?"

"I am."

Cat smiled and picked the chain up from the table. "This chain symbolizes your birth into The Order."

He raised it up, and Banit leaned forward so

it could be placed around his neck. Then Cat picked up the Bible and held it out. "Place your hand on the Bible."

Banit did as he was told, placing his right hand on the Bible, his eyes locked onto Cat's eyes.

"Now repeat after me: 'I'—your name—'with this oath, swear with my life to uphold The Order. To obey and follow all its rules and to always strive to better the principles it is founded upon and to walk in their deeper meanings.'"

After Banit repeated the oath, Cat placed the Bible down and moved on to the bullet. He picked it up, then moved over to the bowl of ashes, where he dipped the tip of the bullet inside. Narrowing his eyebrows, he looked Banit directly in the eyes. Cat put the tip of the bullet on Banit's forehead, making an imprint with the ashes. "May this bullet strike you dead should you violate The Order."

After putting the bullet down, Cat thrust his hand in the bowl of ashes looking for something. After a few seconds, his hand emerged with a needle between his thumb and forefinger. "Your right hand please." Cat took hold of Banit by the wrist and turned his hand over, palm up. A glint of light caught the needle's point before Cat plunged it into his friend's pointer finger.

Their eyes pierced each other's as they stared into each other's soul. Drops of blood trickled off Banit's finger into the bowl. "May your blood turn to ashes should you violate The Order of Thieves."

Both men looked at each other and smiled after the ritual was complete. Cat then walked around the table and hugged his friend. "Welcome, my brother," was all he said.

They walked to a door that led down to the basement. As they descended the steps, Cat flicked on the switches, illuminating the cavernous rooms.

"Welcome to The Lodge," Cat said. It would serve as a headquarters for the team to initiate new members and to discuss all business. It was also where their training would begin, where they would learn the tools of the craft.

Cat had remodeled the house with all the equipment he would need to train new inductees. The floors were tiled with a black-and-white polka-dot design similar to those in a Masonic temple. The colors represented duality—the positive and negative forces that govern the universe, but at The Lodge they were used to symbolize the two thieves that were crucified beside Jesus. Six chairs formed a circle in the middle of the room, with a small table in the right corner. Cat opened a closet in the back of the room and pulled out a large metal case with a handle on top. He opened the case and began to unload its contents on the table: a .45-caliber handgun, duct tape, a watch, a screwdriver, wire cutters, a piece of wooden two-by-four, a crowbar, and a small pouch filled with marbles. Reaching into the case again, he pulled out a shoe box. Cat opened the box to reveal black masks and black gloves. He handed a set to Banit and pulled out a set for himself. They both put on the masks and gloves.

Cat faced the table and explained, "From the mask and gloves to the crowbar, these are the tools of the craft. You will at some point need one or all of these to pull off a jux. It is extremely important that you learn to use each of these tools properly and effectively. Each of them has a symbolic and deeper meaning that is directly related to how a man of The Order should live his life. These meanings are not fully developed. I'm hoping that you'll help me develop them as The Order continues to grow."

Cat introduced Banit to the tools and explained the significance of each. With miniature models of homes and their interiors, Cat demonstrated the use of each tool in various parts of the household. He pointed at the gun and told

Banit to pick it up. Banit did as instructed and handed it over to his mentor.

"A gun commands respect and a mask conceals your identity," Cat explained.

The training had begun. So as not to confuse Banit or overload him with too much on the first session, Cat decided to wrap it up. He wanted his new initiate to take in all the events of the day and think about them. As they made their way out, Cat pointed to another inscription, this time on the back side of the altar.

"Read that," he said.

"'There is no honor among thieves,'" Banit read aloud.

"Remember it."

They left The Lodge and headed toward Cat's place.

"Yo, homey, I gotta ask you, let's just say after taking me through all that today, I decided I didn't wanna be a part of the whole thing. What would happen?" Banit was curious as the night air made him consider going to jail. He had always been a hard worker. He remembered how lucky he felt the day he became the super of Cat's building. The rent-free apartment gave him a great deal of security. He had small dreams and was thinking that this might be too much for him. But even though his dreams were small, his desire for money was big.

"Is that what you've decided?" asked Cat.

"Nah, not at all . . . I definitely wants to fuck with this. Me really like you whole setup. But, you know, I was just wondering."

"I told you to remember that inscription you read on the way out." Cat smiled, looking over at his friend. "That's what it's all about."

"Now just what the fuck is that supposed to mean?"

Cat didn't bother to answer Banit's question. He knew that Banit already had the answer. Going into this whole thing, Cat had already made up his mind: he would indeed have to kill his friend if he decided not to be a part of The Order. Cat had given it plenty of thought the entire time he was putting it all together. Cat knew, from experiences in Jamaica, the nature of the business. He knew that you could never completely trust anyone. But you couldn't watch your own back constantly, without help. You have to sleep and you need some sort of comfort and peace of mind.

To recruit additional members, Banit introduced Cat to his cousin Ozzi, who had just come home from a five-year prison bid. To stay clean, Ozzi worked odd jobs that didn't pay much. He was becoming increasingly impatient with this whole idea of working for chump change and began looking for the right hustle. Ozzi was of average stature, not very muscular, but he did a daily workout and kept in shape. He could easily have defended himself but chose a different route. In jail, he was known for his cunning and devious ways. Other inmates stayed away from him because of his reputation. They heard stories of how he arranged the demise of his enemies. He was calculating and manipulated situations where guards and other inmates would dispose of his enemies for him.

Cat met with Ozzi and thought he'd fit in just fine. Cat sensed an air of leadership in him and initiated him as the third member of The Order.

Cat decided to take his two soldiers out on an actual jux to make Ozzi's and Banit's inductions official. Beforehand, he decided to hold an impromptu question-and-answer session. He told them to forget everything they might have known about pulling off a jux when offering their responses. Banit and Ozzi gave Cat their undivided attention.

"What is the most important thing in pulling off a jux?"

"Making sure the information given is correct," said Banit.

"Making sure the people inside are tied up tightly," said Ozzi.

"And using the proper tools," said Banit.

"The most important thing in pulling off a jux," Cat instructed, "is getting away."

He let them know that it did not matter if you scored or not; if you can't get away, then nothing matters. Reaping the rewards from a job was the main focus. It's what The Order was based upon. This made getting away crucial.

"What is the first and last thing you plan in a jux?"

Banit and Ozzi paused a bit too long, making Cat roar, "Getting away! Getting away! Nothing is to stand in the way of getting away. Firing your gun should always be a last resort, but don't hesitate when it comes to making your escape. If a cop is standing in your way, then he is to be fired upon. If the time permits, fire a warning shot to frighten someone and let them know you mean business. If they are not deterred, then lay them down and make your escape."

"Why not take the arrest and do the time for a lesser charge instead of killing a cop and getting life in prison?" asked Ozzi.

"I can understand why you would ask that question," Cat replied, "since you have already done time. But I don't think you are trying to go back to prison, are you?"

"Oh, hell no!"

"My point exactly." Cat then paused for a

moment, garnering Banit's and Ozzi's full attention. "More importantly, if you go at a jux with that type of mind-set, then there's a greater chance something will go wrong because you'll miss something crucial in the planning phase of the jux. If that kind of situation should arise, your moves would be indecisive because you didn't think that part through. It also means that you don't take your job seriously, putting yourself and the rest of the team at risk.

"Now if you know that you are prepared to kill a cop and understand the seriousness of it, then you will instead take every precaution not to alert them. Keep this in mind: Juxing is a craft. A craft that needs to be sacred to you. Getting arrested means that you can no longer practice your craft. Just think about a lawyer who spends all that time and money in law school, takes the bar exam, passes, then gets arrested and convicted on a felony rap. He can no longer practice his craft in a court of law. How do you think he would feel?" A feeling Cat knew well since his engineering dreams were never realized. "To get arrested is a direct disrespect to the craft and to The Order."

Both Banit and Ozzi sat and listened attentively as Cat schooled them.

"The second thing in a jux is this: If you believe before going in that you're going to have to fire off a shot, then you need to call the jux off until you're able to create a scenario where you'd have complete control of the situation. We're in the business of stealing, not killing. I emphasize that we should avoid killing at all cost. Third, be prepared mentally as well as physically. When I say physically, I don't mean having the tools required for the job. What I mean is that your mind and body must be prepared for anything. You must be prepared to take a man down without the use of your gun. Be prepared to run for miles, to scale the highest fences, hang on to a pole or bars for long periods of time, and even hold your breath until the second before you pass out. So after tonight, we will be spending a lot of time in the gym upstairs. You got it?"

Banit and Ozzi nodded.

"Let the juxing begin."

For their first outing, Cat selected an empty house. He only wanted to see how Ozzi and Banit handled their tools and to test their awareness of their surroundings. They gained entry with a flathead screwdriver through a sliding storm window in the basement. Ozzi stuck the screwdriver into the groove of the sliding track and tilted it back until the window was easy to lift out, just as in their training sessions.

Banit was the lookout as Ozzi stuck his head in looking for signs of movement. They moved in quickly, picked up the bounty, and left without the problem of someone being in the house. Cat was pleased with how his men stepped up to the challenge and the success of their run.

With the art of juxing down, Cat thought it was time to teach them how to steal cars and marksmanship, in case they needed to shoot. He warned them never to take their own car on a jux to avoid the risk of the vehicle's being traced back to them. They hot-wired cars for practice and dumped them. He then took them out into the open fields by Kennedy and La Guardia airports where they practiced their marksmanship in the dark. With their artillery cocked, he instructed them to wait for the landings and take-offs of the planes to muffle the sound of gunfire.

A dog kennel nearby where the airport security hounds were housed reminded him to show the members how to deal with dogs.

"Dogs are able to sense fear on a human so you must never show it. In the event that you are attacked by a dog, you must fight it straight up like you would a man. His nose is his weak point, therefore aim for it with everything you've got," Cat explained.

Planning the getaway was next. Where you parked your car in relation to the target's house and outrunning the cops were extremely important.

"Always try to park on the block behind the house, and if possible try to be directly behind it. When running from the police, never run on the streets, which is a cardinal rule. If you happen to get lucky and lose the cops, they can always pick up your trail if you were spotted by someone who was looking out their window. You can be sure they will assist the cops by pointing out the direction in which you fled. Always run through backyards and over fences. If you can picture this in your head, then you will see the need for being able to scale fences and fighting off dogs, because there is a chance of you running into one of these situations during a getaway."

The training was followed by a string of three more empty-house jobs. A few days later, it was time to try a location with occupants. Their target was a low-level weed dealer. Cat decided to make his targets other criminals. He felt it would make the cops less interested in trying to catch The Order.

Cat knew they'd get some small change in robbing the dealer, providing that everything ran smoothly. They gained easy entry through a ground-floor window that was left open. The dread was in his kitchen cooking when the inductees crept up on him. Cat followed behind with no real intention of getting involved. He checked out their moves. By the time the dread saw the men, he was on the kitchen floor with guns pointed at his face. They gave him no time or chance to react, exactly as Cat had taught them.

After hog-tying him, they searched the house. Twenty-one pounds of dro and $12,000 were found. Both Ozzi and Banit were happy with their find and were ready to leave. Cat told them their search wasn't over. He reminded them that until the deeds to the property were found, they hadn't done a thorough enough search. It took them another hour before they found the papers in a fireproof box along with some jewelry.

"Understand now why it's important to not end the search till you find those papers? Look at what you would have missed," Cat reprimanded.

Now they were ready for some of the bigger jobs that Cat had lined up. Cat decided it was time to introduce them to the "rush." This was the most dangerous of the jux because the circumstances changed quickly.

It was a last resort whenever a jux could not be taken by gaining entry through a window. You wait until the target is entering the premises, run up on your victim, and force the person into the house. It's tricky, something Cat learned in the military, and only for professionals. He took the men on a few practice sessions before they tackled the real thing.

The target was a young hustler named Dime. Cat had set his sights on him about eight months ago, while Banit and Ozzi were still in training. Cat was putting together an entertainment system, so he went to an electronics store two blocks from City Hall in downtown Manhattan in search of new speakers. While there, he noticed Dime talking to one of the store clerks about a floor-model television. The salesman ran through all the features for him. It was their best, biggest, and most expensive model in stock. What interested Cat was how Dime would have that kind of money. Clearly the TV was for someone who had money to burn. Cat played the conversation close, even telling the clerk and Dime how impressive the set looked. Dime was sold on the television. Cat watched as Dime paid for his set.

Cat's interest only grew when Dime pulled out his bankroll. He had the whole $4,000 in cash and much more, secured by a golden money clip with several diamonds encrusted in it. Cat knew what had to be done. *Play this bitch close.* The salesperson handed Dime a proof-of-purchase form on which he wrote his name and address for delivery. Unfortunately Cat was unable to get close enough to see what his new-found victim wrote. His hopes came alive when he overheard the salesman say the TV would arrive in two days, but Dime wanted it delivered that day. Dime was used to giving orders and was willing to pay extra to have it done. The clerk had no authority to make such arrangements. A manager was called up front. With the extra payment, the manager assured Dime that the television would be delivered by 4 p.m. that day. That was all Cat needed to set up the jux. He decided to follow the delivery truck.

Cat waited in his car until he saw the deliverymen loading the TV onto the truck from the side entrance of the store. He followed them to Brooklyn Heights. Cat never took much interest in Brooklyn because of its layout. Too heavily populated, too few highways, and the majority of homes were too close together. The truck turned onto Orange Street in Brooklyn Heights and stopped at the second house on the block. Cat drove past. He went around the block slowly and came back around. As he drove past the truck this time, he noticed Dime come out of the house to meet the driver. Cat drove on, making a mental note.

Later that night, Cat returned to case the

house. There were no weak points of entry. Bars were cemented into the walls outside every window of the home. Crowbars and two-by-fours were useless here. Although the bars could be sawn through, the neighboring house was too close. Even if they were able to get in on a night Dime wasn't home, they would run the risk of alerting neighbors with the sound of sawing. The windows even had alarm tape on them, and the alarm box was on the roof. The box could easily be disabled, but it would be impossible getting to it without being seen. *With all this security, this bitch has to be protecting something valuable, and I doubt it is a woman.*

Cat needed to find out more about Dime and his movements. Cat went through his mail and found out his real name was Perry Adams. He was a hustler, not a street peddler. He did his business exclusively through the clubs in the city. He was a VIP distributor. Models, actors, and business executives were his customers. This meant that his movements would be easy to track.

Cat wanted to test Banit and Ozzi's information-gathering skills on this jux. Cat showed them where Dime lived and told them to track him and learn as much as they possibly could. For the next two weeks, they staked him out, first in a van that Cat had bought secondhand, then in Banit's station wagon. They paid attention to every detail when keeping an eye on Dime. A daily report was brought back to Cat, who already knew most of the information. Once Cat was satisfied with The Order's surveillance, he decided they were ready. In two days they would commit the jux.

The day prior to the jux, Cat opened his door, and to his surprise Banit and Ozzi were standing before him dressed in suits and trench coats. They were carrying duffel bags that were filled and obviously heavy.

"Sup with the suits?" Cat asked.

They walked into his living room and dropped the bags on the floor.

Banit said, "We one big rass surprise for you." He then knelt down and opened one of the bags.

Cat's eyes widened with surprise. "What the fuck?"

"We jux the boy Dime this morning posing as police. While we was watching him, we noticed the past two Thursdays, he left his house at ten o'clock and drove to the post office. We followed him in the second time and saw that he bought a money order and put it into an envelope and dropped it in the mailbox. We decided to chance that this was a pattern and took a gamble that he would do the same this Thursday, which he did. As soon as he came out the house and was about to enter his car, we were waiting in the driveway for him. He was so caught off guard that he simply froze and did not know what to do or say. It was as if he was waiting for this moment. We put him in the van and cuffed him in the back before he could realize we were fakes. We took his keys and went inside, and this is what we came back with."

Banit pointed to the bags. Ozzi reached into his coat pocket. He felt around a bit, then came back out with a piece of paper. "And here is the deed." He held it up with a smile of pride.

Cat folded his arms across his chest. Then a smile flashed across his face. He nodded his head toward his men. He was proud.

"Fifty-two keys of coke there and maybe a halfa million in cash," said Ozzi.

"I'm very impressed," said Cat. "In fact, I'm more than impressed . . . you and him do a good rassclaat job."

FIVE

Both Prince and James were longtime friends of Ozzi's. He brought the both of them to meet Cat, so he could get a feel for them. Ozzi did not tell them the nature of the meeting beforehand; this way, if Cat was not feeling either of them, they could be turned away from The Order without any hard feelings.

Ozzi invited them for a night out with Cat and Banit at a club in the city. The Lemon Lounge, located in an old warehouse, was in the Meatpacking District. It was the first time The Order had been out to party in a long time. Ozzi, Cat, and Banit were dressed to the nines, having used some of their money to purchase fresh, top-of-the-line designer suits. When they moved through the club together, some women got whiplash just trying to keep their eyes on the men as long as possible. It was an occasion to see three fine brothers dressed to impress. Prince and James, not as pulled together, lagged behind unnoticed.

Cat walked up to the bar with the confidence of a millionaire and ordered a round of drinks for everyone at the bar. Word spread quickly throughout the club, and people crowded around the bar screaming drink orders to the bartenders. Cat stepped aside gleaming with his newfound power. Prince and James looked on in envy. Once the crowd settled back to their dancing, the crew went upstairs and took a table near the DJ. They ordered Cristal and drank bottle after bottle. Women would pass by frequently, giving the men seductive glances. After a few drinks, the men moved about the club freely, everybody except Cat, who sat at a table paying attention to Prince's and James's every action.

Prince spent most of the night on the dance floor, tiring one woman out, then moving on to the next. James, who had a girlfriend at home, amused himself by looking at all the beautiful women, but dared not speak to them or touch them. He was leaning against the bar just smiling and looking at the ladies.

Harmless and obedient, Cat believed, considering James's woman could control him even when she wasn't around. After going through several women in his neighborhood, James had met "the one." Symone was what some men would call a gold digger, but to James she was the woman of his dreams. She had the unique skill of keeping him in line, which meant being devoted only to her. She was clever and had a way of telling him what he could and could not do so that he thought it was his idea.

If this man could be trained by a woman, imagine what Cat could do with him. Cat was satisfied with what he had seen in both men and began to relax. Not only did he pay attention to the people in the crowd, Cat was also enthralled by the workers—the bartenders, the busboys, the waitresses, and the security guards. He felt thankful that his days as an hourly wage employee were over. Cat noticed how hard the people in the club worked, and he never wanted to go back to that kind of existence. It was thrilling to him to have been able to purchase drinks for everyone at the bar, knowing that it did not make a dent in his wallet but made a huge impression on the clubgoers.

When the next woman passed, Cat motioned for her to take a seat. Cat admired her beauty and was free in complimenting the long-legged, large-breasted woman. He ordered more champagne and a few appetizers for their enjoyment. She was clearly taken by Cat's kindness, but he left her at the club wanting more.

After initiating Prince and James, Cat fell back from an active role in the crew. He hardly went out with The Order, except when he felt out of touch, bored, or when he wanted to see if everyone was keeping his skills sharp. He fell back to almost exclusively finding the jobs. Though all of the men were involved with scoping out targets, Cat checked them out to see if they were a worthy jux.

Ozzi now stepped up in Cat's place. He was responsible for overseeing The Lodge and taking the lead role on each jux. They were able to rob most of their targets multiple times. They would just wait until their victims built their stash up again. Some of them eventually got tired of being robbed and went to the cops. They robbed one dealer five times before he went to the police for help. The police didn't help him any. The Order robbed him twice more after that. His calls to the police eventually led to his own arrest because, while watching out for the robbers, the police observed his drug business as well. It was futile to attempt to stop the jux.

James was the fifth member to join The Order. He was the nephew of Prince, who was close to his nephew. While Prince was upstate doing a three-year stretch in a state prison, James took care of him, regularly sending commissary money and packages. When he got home, James took Prince shopping and got him looking like a million dollars.

James was devoted to his uncle because he had never forgotten that his uncle Prince was kind to him as a child. Prince was the first to take James to a movie theater when he arrived from Jamaica. It was also James's first time riding a subway train, which excited him.

Since his arrival in the States, James had been pretty much a loner, except for the time he spent with Symone and a few boys from his old neighborhood. Though he had some friends and knew a lot of people, no one knew exactly what criminal element supported his endeavors. It was as though he had an aptitude for the jux. His actions were always smooth and deliberate. He also possessed something that others did not. He had honesty and sincerity in the things he did—traits that attracted Cat's admiration.

James and Prince moved well together as a team. Because they were family, they would naturally go that extra mile to look out for each other's back.

Cloud was the last to join the crew. Banit brought him in. They had met in prison.

Banit did a year on Rikers Island fighting an attempted-murder case. He was pulled over by the police one evening for doing forty-five in a 25 mph residential zone. The officer ran his license and discovered it was suspended. Banit was immediately arrested. While at the precinct, he was picked out in a lineup as the shooter in an attempted-murder case. Two men were arguing and one of them pulled out a gun and shot the other. An elderly lady looking out her window from six stories up identified Banit as the shooter. After a year of hearings, the judge decided to throw the case out, on the grounds that the lineup was not conducted in accordance with the law.

Cloud and Banit became close while they were incarcerated. When the Bloods tried to press Banit for his chain one day, Cloud, a stranger to Banit at the time, stepped up and vouched for him. Banit was grateful. They were mad cool after that. They spoke of ways of coming up in the streets together and decided to keep in contact when they touched down on the town.

Prince and James were keeping really busy. They were firmly ensconced members of The Order. They did a lot of jux as a team. Their kinship made their bond a natural. Often, when business wasn't being conducted, they hung out together. Prince and James were the only ones who were allowed to act independently of the frat, since they were doing robberies before they were inducted. Cat also had more confidence in their skills than those of the rest of his team. Prince and James always seemed to shine.

Another reason Cat allowed Prince and James to do their thing independently of the frat was to throw off any cops that might be sniffing around. One of the rules of The Lodge was to never do a jux in an apartment building. There were just too many tenants; too much potential that they could be spotted. However, James and Prince did these jobs anyway and at any time of the day.

AT ABOUT ONE O'CLOCK ONE afternoon James got a call.

"Yush," he answered.

"Yes, yes, a me," Prince replied.

"What up?"

"What up, Nephew? Me have some ting."

"Word?" James asked with a smile on his face.

"You remember where me friend Dubs live?"

"Yes, me remember."

"Meet me there," Prince said, and hung up.

Fifteen minutes later, James pulled up in front of a building where his uncle was waiting. Prince and Dubs were outside leaning on the hood of a parked car.

James stepped out to greet them. "What up?" he asked, giving them the half hug.

"What's up, lil' neph? Hear dis, Dub's man got some ting for us."

"Who dat?" asked James.

"He'll be here in a few to give us the rundown," Dubs replied. "He got at me yesterday 'bout it, and I told him I was gonna holla at y'all 'bout it 'cause he said he couldn't do it. Motherfucker knows him probably, know what I'm sayin'?"

A young man by the name of Allen came walking around the corner a few minutes later. He greeted everybody, then all four men got into Prince's car, parked nearby. James and Dubs sat in the back, while Prince and Allen sat up front.

"Who dat?" Allen asked apprehensively.

"He cool . . . he rolling with us," said Prince.

"What!?" Allen shot back. "Nah, fuck that! I already told you, no more than two niggaz on this shit. Now you trying to tell me this shit is gonna be a four-way split? Hell no, I ain't wid it."

"Man, chill out and be easy," said Dubs.

"Nah, nigga, you be easy," said Allen, pointing his finger. "If two niggaz can't get it done, then that's a wrap. I'ma find someone else to do this shit, it's that simple."

"Listen, that's my nephew, and he official," said Prince.

"Fuck that, I don't care who he be, I ain't splitting my share any further."

"Look, kid, you bugging out now over some bullshit. . . . He don't want much . . . he just looking for some rent money, that's all," said Prince, playing the diplomat. "Plus that's my sister Marcia's son. He cool."

Marcia used to babysit Allen when he was a boy. Prince knew mentioning her name would sway Allen's judgment.

Allen shared the details of the jux. The target was a hustler named Bell, originally from Corona, who moved out to an apartment building in Flushing, Queens, after doing a state bid. Bell met a good connect on the inside, and now Bell was moving about six bricks a week.

When Bell came home from prison, he weighed about 240. He was just a shadow of his former self these days, weighing in at about 115 pounds. He was a different man now. Physically, no one would even recognize him. Bell had contracted a stomach virus and was dying. He wasn't sure when or how he caught the virus; all he knew was that it was slowly and painfully eating him alive. Doctors diagnosed him and gave him maybe a year to live. Because of his virus, Bell lacked the strength to do all the running around. He brought in his nephew Slim to conduct his day-to-day business.

That was Bell's big mistake. No one but Slim knew where his uncle lived. Allen and Slim were good friends, and although he never told Allen where his uncle lived, Slim did brag to him about the amount of drugs he was moving for Bell.

Allen began to scheme more after Bell's nephew bragged and started flashing his cash around. Allen began to clock every move Slim made. Allen noticed that it was pretty much the same pattern every day. He followed him until he tracked him to Bell's building. Allen watched the building for several days to find out what time Slim walked the dog and took out the trash. Once he got that pattern down, it was time to call in some help, and Dubs was his man.

The plan was to grab and tie up the nephew on his way in or out of the apartment, then rush in. Dubs and Allen also called on Prince. But there was one problem. Whatever was about to go down, it was critical that Bell not see their faces. Since Bell knew Allen, he would easily link all three of them together. Allen didn't care how they did it, just as long as things couldn't be traced back to him. Although Bell himself couldn't physically bring harm to any of them, he had powerful friends who could. Prince recommended that the crew use his nephew James. Bell didn't know him. He could disable Bell and his nephew Slim before the other two men entered, then they would be good. They could come in and help with the searching while James kept Bell and his nephew secured.

Two days later everything was set and everyone was in position to go. Prince, Dubs, and James were poised in the staircase waiting for their moment. Slim had just returned from walking the dog and was heading back into the apartment. The crew was waiting for him to come back out with the garbage, as was his routine. The moment was here, and James was in position to jump Slim at gunpoint. When the door opened, instead of moving out on them, it seemed like James froze up. James gripped his piece tighter. Prince stared at James. Prince could hear Bell and his nephew conversing. Prince whispered to James, "What up?"

James put a finger over his lips signaling his uncle to be easy. Dubs looked irritated.

Bell's nephew exited the apartment with the garbage bag in his hand while Bell stood at the door. The elevator was right beside Bell's apartment, so they talked some more while Slim waited for the elevator to arrive. Slim got on, and before the elevator doors shut, he yelled out what time he would be back tomorrow. Suddenly, James took off running from the stairs and down the hall at lightning speed. He closed in perfectly on Bell. Slim did not notice a thing as he was going down on the elevator. It was less risky not having to disable two men. They only had to contend with feeble, scrawny Bell.

James came charging through the apartment door just before it closed, knocking Bell over and laying him facedown on the ground.

"Don't fucking move or make a sound if you wanna live," James commanded as he threw a rag over Bell's head to cover his eyes. Prince and Dubs stormed the apartment, checking for other occupants. Dubs signaled that the coast was clear. James helped Bell to his feet and led him to the bathroom, where he made him sit down inside the bathtub. He tied his hands behind his back and questioned him about the location of the drugs and the money. He warned Bell he would be killed if they found anything more than what he said was there.

Bell told them where everything was. Prince stood outside the bathroom listening. Prince and Dubs bagged up all the cocaine, money, guns, jewelry, and some expensive camera equipment while James kept an eye on Bell. When they were finished and ready to leave, James told them to go ahead, he would catch up with them in the car. He didn't want the three of them to leave together and bring attention to themselves. He gave them a five-minute head start.

Bell looked bad.

"I see you're not in such good shape. So I'm going to leave you some slack in the cord so you can free yourself instead of waiting here for someone to find you," James said.

"Good lookin' out, man," was all Bell said.

James was the last to enter the hotel room at La Guardia that Allen had booked earlier in the evening. Allen was happy like a pig in shit to see all of them, which meant everything went smoothly. Prince, Dubs, and Allen began counting out the money and splitting up the cocaine. Meanwhile James collected their guns and put them in a bag beside him. He walked back over to the other men, leaning against the dresser with his gun safely secured at his waist. Allen counted out $1,000 in cash and handed it to James.

"What's this?" James asked, looking down at the money.

"Your cut," Allen replied.

James looked over to Prince, who looked back. Prince then turned to Allen and said, "Yo, listen, man, he gotta get an equal share."

"What!? What you talkin' 'bout he gotta get an equal share? You said the nigga only needed some rent money. Now you talkin' this equal-share shit? This that same shit I was talkin' 'bout from the jump."

"Yo, you buggin' out again, man, you lettin' this money and some greed shit get to you," said Dubs.

"Ain't shit gettin' to me! I told y'all niggaz that I wasn't with splittin' my share any further, and now y'all niggaz is pullin' some flimflam shit after the fact. Hell no! Now you wanna tell me I'm on some shit?" Allen asked, pointing to himself. "Nah, y'all niggaz is on some shit, not me."

"Dog, you really buggin' the fuck out." Prince pointed to his nephew James. "If it wasn't for him, none of this shit would have came off."

Allen had a puzzled look on his face. "I gave y'all niggaz a perfect plan, all y'all had to do was follow it. So don't try dat shit on me. I'm too smart fo' dat."

"Nigga, ain't nobody trying anything. If it wasn't for him, we couldn't have pulled that plan off. We could have risked blowin' all our covers, including yours, nigga."

Dubs backed up Prince, saying, "That's real talk, Allen. The nigga was the first one in and the last one to leave."

After they told Allen how it all went down, he had a change of mind and heart. He was impressed with James's movements, so he gave him his equal share. Prince was glad they came to that understanding. He knew his nephew wouldn't have stood for anything other than that. He could read the boy's mind. James would have had to stick up everybody in the room, even Prince, to make it look legit. Later they'd meet up and he'd give his uncle his cut.

The four men split up the catch and were on their way. Allen had his own car. Dubs got in with Prince, and James drove away in his own. They pulled out of the hotel parking lot one after the other. Prince was heading back to Corona to drop off Dubs. Allen and James were heading in the opposite direction. As they drove along the service road toward the highway, James beeped his horn, signaling Allen to pull over. He did. Both vehicles were stopped and James got out and walked toward Allen's car. Two cars were in the distance driving their way. As James got to Allen's door and leaned over, the first car drove by.

"What's up?" asked Allen.

"Listen, man, I just wanted to thank you for cutting me in on the whole thing."

Allen looked at the young boy and smiled. "It's nothin', dog, you deserve it, it was the least I could do."

Allen turned to see the second car drive

by them. When he turned back, he was staring down the barrel of James's gun. Allen's eyes opened wide in surprise.

Bang!

One shot rang out, blowing in Allen's head, sending bits of brain and skull all over his passenger seat. The car began to roll as Allen's foot lightened on the brakes. James quickly put half his body through the window reaching for the gearshift. He put the car in park and brought it to a stop. He popped the trunk and took out the bags that held Allen's cut and his piece. Then James got in his car and was out.

SIX

Cat wasn't sure if it was instincts or paranoia, but something told him it would be a good idea to keep everyone out of sight for a while. After the killing of that man and his lady on their last jux, another shooting was sure to bring heat.

Allen's death made Cat really nervous. For a moment he even thought about breaking up The Order, but he knew that if he did, no one would have a reason to keep quiet. He also wouldn't know their moves or what they were up to. He decided to just wait things out. He called a meeting at The Lodge and informed everyone that there would be no more juxes for a while. They all had enough money to hold them down.

Cat's plan was to shut down The Lodge for

now and see what played out. Within a year, he would make a decision on their next move. If it was safe enough to open up shop again, then they would regroup. He instructed them to clean everything out and leave no trace behind. Cat pulled Ozzi and Banit aside and told them to keep a close eye on Cloud to ensure he didn't pull a jux on his own. He was the least known out of everyone. With that, the meeting came to a close.

The next night, Ozzi returned to The Lodge to collect the rest of his belongings. He gathered up his stuff and headed for the door. He stopped cold at the sound of police radios. A chill ran through his spine and froze him dead in his tracks. He looked out the window to his right and saw movements outside, silhouetted against the curtains. Dropping his bag, Ozzi pulled his gun from his waist and dropped down to a squat position. A knock at the door tightened the already nervous sensation gripping the pit of his stomach.

"Shit," he said under his breath.

Ozzi began to move toward the back of The Lodge, into the kitchen. He went to the window and moved the curtain to the side just a bit to see what was out there. There was nothing that resembled police.

"Fuck it!"

Ozzi lifted the window. A cool breeze rushed in, sending the curtains flapping. He stuck his head outside, looked around toward the back of the house. No sign of the police. There was another aggressive knock. It sounded like the typical police knock. Ozzi put his foot on top of the radiator and hoisted half his body through the window. The coast was clear. He maneuvered the rest of his body outside. He crept to the side of the house and looked around the corner toward the front, where he saw police cruisers and vans lined up outside. This wasn't looking good. If he was going to make a break for it, now was definitely the time. He turned and headed for the back fence. Just as he got to the fence, ready to scale it, he heard those dreaded words: "Freeze, asshole!"

Ozzi recalled what Cat had said about firing on the police to get away. Ozzi spun around and took aim. Five officers had walked up the other side of the house. The lead officer was hit in the neck from Ozzi's rounds. The second officer was hit in the thigh. All five officers managed to fire off several rounds, but amazingly none hit Ozzi. The cops scrambled for cover as Ozzi jumped over the fence. He fell to the ground but rolled over still firing off shots. That's when he felt a burning sensation in the back of his legs. He felt the bullet graze his right thigh, then he felt as though he were hit by a hammer in his right buttock. After a quick exchange of gunfire, Ozzi ran out of ammo and the cops closed in. Ozzi lay still on the ground as they approached with caution. One officer kicked the gun away from his hand. He was still alive with fourteen bullet wounds. One of the officers put his boot on Ozzi's neck and pressed down to cut off his breathing. Another officer ran over and pushed the cop with the boot on his neck. Semiconscious now, Ozzi heard one cop say to the other, "What the fuck do you think you're doing? We been tracking these guys for a long time. We won't be able to get information from a dead man about the others. We should have busted up their meeting the other night."

Miraculously, Ozzi found the strength to lift his head. Then his eyes widened in disbelief. He was looking at the officer that pushed the other one away.

"You," Ozzi managed to mutter, "you fucking tr-tr . . ." And those were Ozzi's last words.

OZZI WAS SUPPOSED TO PHONE Banit when he was done retrieving his things from The Lodge, but the entire day passed with no calls. Banit called Cat, who reported that he hadn't heard anything either. Something was up. Then Banit called Cloud, but his service picked up. Banit left a message to get in touch as soon as possible. Banit decided to swing by The Lodge. He drove by and kept driving. No need to stop to realize police had been there. Quickly, he relayed what he had seen to Cat and Prince. They tried to get ahold of Cloud to warn him as well, but still no answer. They left him warning messages nonetheless. Prince got to James and let him know what was up. He told him he was leaving town and advised him to do the same.

Everyone was scrambling and going his separate way. Prince went to Atlanta to hide out with his mother for a while. James decided he was going to stay put and spend quality time with Symone. After all, he wasn't with the crew for that long. James didn't feel the heat was on him as much as the rest of the guys. Banit decided he could no longer wait on Ozzi, who he assumed escaped and was now in "duckdown mode" like the rest of them.

Banit made a quick stop at his safety-deposit box to get his fake ID and passport. On the way back to his car, he stopped at a pay phone and called Ozzi's mother to see if she'd heard anything from him. The news hit Banit like a freight train. Ozzi was pronounced dead at 2 a.m. that morning, and his wake was in three days. Banit tried calling Cat to tell him, but he was long gone. Cloud got back to Banit the next day, just as he was about to dump his cell phone.

"I've been trying to get at you for the longest, where you been?" barked Banit.

"Man, I been in hiding after I seen all them fucking pigs crawlin' around The Lodge."

"You know what the fuck happened to Ozzi?"

"Nah, what happened?"

"Nigga got killed! His moms said he got shot up by them po-lice. He's dead, yo. I heard the nigga went out blazin'," Banit reported proudly, "but you know those motherfuckers had him outgunned. They said Ozzi fired on them first and hit a few of them. I just wish I was there with him to bang it out with them."

It was hard to believe because you're with someone one day, then he's gone the next. It's just crazy.

There was silence on the line as Cloud took in the news, then he finally said, "Damn, that's some fucked-up shit."

"Word. Imagine how I feel. I'm the nigga that got him into all this shit," Banit said, the guilt weighing heavily on him now.

"Dog, you can't go blaming yourself for shit like this. We all got into this shit fully aware of the dangers. It's fucked-up, but if it wasn't this, then something else woulda got us. At least niggaz got to make some real paper and a motherfucker got a chance to do some living. I don't regret nothing. I don't know 'bout you, dog, but I got the chance to do me, and that's all I'm gonna say on that."

"I guess you right," Banit finally replied. "It's just hard to think of him gone."

"What's up with Cat? Where's that nigga at?"

"I don't know where the fuck that dude at, once he got the news, that was the last anyone heard of him, he was out."

"What about Prince and James?" Cloud asked.

"Same thing with Prince. I don't know 'bout that nigga James. He ain't been around much anyways. Hope Prince let him know the deal."

CAT MADE HIS WAY DOWN to Miami without telling anyone. He stayed in his two-bedroom apartment that he rented the last time he visited the city. He knew better than to call his mother or his sister, both their phones would be tapped. He felt assured that they also knew that at a time like this, they would never hear from him. He had long prepared them for this. The building that he'd bought was in his sister's name and so was The Lodge. His sister, Carroll, was older than him and an accountant, and he had helped her start her own firm. Through her, he was able to wash all of his money. She knew all the places he could hide it. Real estate was the best investment she felt. She purchased other properties for her brother that he didn't even know about. Cat also helped out Carroll's husband with his own auto body shop. They were forever grateful and knew how to look out when it was time.

The other members of The Order knew how to deal with this kind of situation. Prince and James weren't with the fraternity for long, so they were not down with many of the lucrative juxes of the past. They weren't as "caked-up" as the rest of the crew so they had to continue doing their thing in the streets. Before Ozzi's death, he had been able to buy his mother two brownstone buildings in Brooklyn. He also had a house he'd purchased under his son's mother's name. He even had $800,000 in a safety-deposit box that she was able to get to.

Banit's mother died of cancer two years prior to his meeting Cat. His father was in Attica Correctional Facility doing a life sentence for killing a cop. Banit had sent him $15,000 a few months back with a note saying, "Spend it wisely. It should hold you for a while." Banit had the rest of his money stashed in a wall of his janitor's office in Cat's building. He couldn't go back there, so he was trying to figure out a way to get it. He planned on going to Canada, where he had a sister, but he needed to get this money first. There was also Ozzi's funeral, which he felt he should attend. Banit felt responsible for Ozzi's death, and he had to see his boy one last time.

IT WAS ABOUT FIVE THIRTY in the evening and the service was set to begin. Ozzi's mother, son, and son's mother were in attendance along with other family members and friends. Banit stepped out of the taxi, but not before looking in all directions. Everything seemed smooth and normal, no signs that the police were around. Just in case they were there or to come later, he was armed and ready to shoot his way out. He began walking toward the funeral parlor, still looking around for any signs of the cops. He could see none, so he walked up the steps and entered the building.

Ten minutes later Cloud walked in. As he took his shades off, he spotted Banit. Banit had just walked away from viewing the body in the coffin and was about to sit down when he looked toward the door and saw Cloud standing there. He changed direction and headed toward Cloud to greet him. He was somewhat surprised to see Cloud. Never in a million years did he think Cloud would attend Ozzi's funeral. After all, Cloud didn't know Ozzi well enough to take the risk of showing up.

After greeting each other, Cloud and Banit conversed a bit.

"So, tell me, how he look?"

"They did a good job in making him look good for his mother. She's really fucked up over this."

"I can only imagine. What are you planning to do?"

"I'm jetting out of here no later than to-night."

"Where to?"

"Canada, I got a sister there."

"You heard anything from the rest of the team?"

"Naw, nothing, you know them dudes long gone."

"Listen, I gotta show you something. Take this walk with me outside for a minute."

They turned and walked out the double doors with Cloud in the lead. When they got outside, Cloud turned and said, "Brethren, I'm going to miss the fuck outta you."

"I'm gonna miss you, too, brethren."

Cloud then gave Banit a hug. A task force and SWAT team suddenly sprang into action. Van doors burst open and they came pouring out, guns pointed and aimed at the two. At the same moment, the cops inside the building were making their move toward the doors. Banit spotted them over Cloud's shoulder, coming from what seemed to be all directions.

"The fucking cops!" Banit shouted just as Cloud pushed him backward. He felt a tug at his waist as he stumbled back trying to regain his balance. At first, he thought he was hit by a bullet, but he heard no gunshots. He looked down at himself—no blood. He looked at Cloud.

In Cloud's hands was a gun. Banit finally caught his balance, looking bewildered. *What is Cloud doing? What is he doing with my gun?*

"Don't move or try anything stupid, Banit. It's over, there's nowhere to run."

Cloud had disarmed Banit as he pushed him away.

"I know the code you live by, but these men will have you laying dead in a coffin next to your cousin if you try something."

"You loco fuck-face." Banit leaped toward Cloud, realizing that he was working with the cops. His efforts to get at Cloud and break his neck were useless. He was quickly met by the task force, who tackled and brought him to the ground and handcuffed him.

Back at the precinct, in the interrogation room, Banit was handcuffed to a chair. The door opened and in walked Cloud with a folder in his hand and a shield in full display. Banit looked at him as he pulled out the chair on the opposite side of the table and sat down. He sat the folder down in front of him, never taking his eyes off Banit.

"I know you just can't believe it right now," bragged Cloud.

"Fuck you!"

"But this is all real. You are not dreaming, all this is really happening."

"Fuck you!"

"Yes, I'm a cop, I was planted in the cell with you on the Island. Those dudes that pressed you for your chain were also cops. It was all set up in order for me to get close to you—"

"So what, fuck you."

"—gain your trust, and have you bring me into the folds of The Order."

Though Banit continued with the I-don't-give-a-fuck attitude, he was shocked and in disbelief. He felt as though he needed to hear more.

"So, how did you ID me?"

"Amongst the jewelry that you guys lifted off of that mobster on Staten Island was a custom-made watch. There's only one like it in the world. It was made specifically for him by a top Italian jeweler, who also took the time to engrave it with a serial number and a back that only an authorized jeweler can open. You sold the watch to a jeweler who tried to open it, but could not. He in turn decided to run the serial number and found out that it was stolen. The cops were alerted, and this led to a viewing of the jewelry-store surveillance tapes. There was your ugly face selling the watch. So all this crap about you doing forty-five in a twenty-five-mile-per-hour zone was just bullshit. Your license was never suspended. That lady never saw you shoot anyone. All that was nothing but a setup to get close to you. Man, even the fucking judge was in on it."

Cloud looked at Banit and smiled, feeling good, thinking how extravagant the plan was to get in with the gang.

Banit could only sit listening to how he was played for a sucker.

"So here is the deal, my friend."

Banit laughed at Cloud. "Motherfucker, I'm not your friend."

"Oh, yeah, we're no longer friends?" Cloud asked with even more sarcasm in his tone.

Banit laughed even louder and harder.

"I'm really glad you find all this funny, considering the fact that you are totally fucked and will spend the rest of your natural life in prison."

"Yeah?"

"Yes! We are sitting on an airtight case here.

You and OJ's fucking dream team couldn't come up with a strong enough defense to sell to the dumbest jury. No, not with me getting on the stand on the DA's side."

"So go ahead and do what you gotta do, you cocksucking pig."

"Remember, Banit, I was there. I saw it all. I saw you and the rest of those assholes you think are your friends shoot those people in cold blood."

Banit stopped laughing when he heard the last words out of Cloud's sentence.

"That's right, I figured that would get your attention."

"That's bullshit!" Banit screamed, spit spraying from his lips. "You made that happen, you fucked that up."

"I know that, you know that, but who's here to say so? It's my word against yours, and who do you think twelve hardworking, tax-paying citizens are going to believe? A man who runs around every day risking his life to protect them and their property, or a thug like you who goes out every day trying to kill them or take from them? I think you know the fucking answer to that."

"So your case is open-and-shut. Why the fuck you're still talking to me?"

"Because I want to help you help yourself."

"You, the supercop want to help me? Get the fuck outta here."

"There can be light at the end of the tunnel for you. Whadaya say?"

Banit took a deep breath, then looked Cloud straight in the eyes. "Go suck out your mother!"

"Mmm, mm, mm, you shouldn't feel like that, my friend."

Banit began to feel himself getting angrier. He wanted to get his hands on Cloud somehow. He wanted to commit murder.

"You set me up, and killed me cousin, and now you want me for help you lock up me brethren dem? You must loss you frigging mind, yah blood claat."

"All right, have it your way. I have come to know your so-called friends, and I know people like them can't stay in hiding for long. All they need is to see money and they will go for it. I'll get 'em. You can bet that, asshole."

SEVEN

James was now on his own again, back to doing what he did prior to becoming a part of The Order. The difference was that he had acquired new training and experience from running with the crew. He became more organized and more planning went into his jux. He also went for bigger stakes. Vill, who grew up with James, decided to approach him about a jux he had lined up. He told him about a jewelry store he had been casing for a long while, and that he thought they could jux it easily. At first James was not interested, but his girl, Symone, was encouraging, and Vill kept on pressing how easy and safe it would be.

Vill could have got someone else to go with him, but he wanted no one other than James to ride with him on it. He knew James's "gun game" was serious from all the work he had put in around the hood. Plus everyone in the hood knew James as a damn good stickup kid.

"Man, I'm telling you, this thing is a walk in the park, dog!"

"Homeboy, I told you that I don't jux legitimate businesses. To stay underneath the radar of the police I only rob criminals. In my mind it helps to bring justice."

"Yo, at least check it out before you say no."

"All right, we'll check it out tomorrow. After that you can get the fuck off my back."

The following day they drove by the store. It was located in the city by the Fifty-ninth Street bridge that crosses over the East River from Queens to Manhattan. James parked around the corner. They got out and put a quarter in the meter, then walked around the corner by the jewelry store. They walked slowly, looking into all the windows of the stores they passed until they got to the jewelry store. They stopped and pretended to be looking at the jewelry on display in the window. They had a clear view into the store, which wasn't that big. Two customers were at the counter. While they were looking in, a lady walked into the store. James noticed that she didn't have to be buzzed in. He turned to Vill and asked, "So you say you been casing it?"

"Yeah, that's right."

"You been inside yet?"

"Yeah, three times."

"Did you see any cameras in there?"

"Nah, I didn't see any when I was in there."

"All right, come on."

They began walking back down the block. James was looking around at all the stores on the blocks as they passed them. They walked about five blocks, then crossed the street and walked back in the direction they came from doing the same thing again. James was checking out the other stores and the layout of the area. They then crossed the street and went back around the corner to their car and got in. James drove about fifteen blocks, then suddenly began to slow down. "Exactly what am I looking for?" James asked himself out loud.

"What you talking about?"

"Yes, a movie theater."

"A movie theater? What you want with a movie theater?"

"Nigga, just chill and hold the tail and let me fuck the cow."

James then made a U-turn and drove back in the direction from which they came. After thinking things over, he agreed that it would be a good and easy jux. His only worry was Vill, who was no kin of his. If they got caught, the chance of Vill ratting on him was more than likely. With that in mind, James made their escape his main focus. Everything had to be planned to a tee, nothing could be allowed to go wrong. Vill had to get away safely to ensure both their safety.

The next day they went to Foot Locker and bought two tear-away basketball warm-up suits. They then went to a little Chinese store and bought a mask and gloves for Vill. From there James drove by the store again. He wanted to see if he might have missed anything. Satisfied, he turned to Vill and told him, "It's going down tomorrow, so be ready. Also make sure that you keep this shit between you and me."

Vill said nothing in response. He simply bopped his head while deep in thoughts of his own.

James added, "Not even your fucking brother."

The following day James picked up Vill and they drove to New Jersey. They pulled into a parking lot and drove around for a couple of minutes. James stopped suddenly.

"Perfect!" he said, looking to his right at a green Nissan Maxima. He pulled up next to it and parked.

"Reach in the back and pass me that bag on the seat."

Vill did as he was told.

"Okay, when I get out, you get behind the wheel and follow me."

Vill nodded and climbed behind the wheel when James exited the car with the bag in his hand. James leaned against the passenger door of the Maxima after taking a slim jim from his bag. He stuck it down between the window and the door frame and maneuvered it until the door came unlocked. He then opened the door and got in. He took a pulley out of the bag and assembled it. He screwed it into the ignition, and with three slaps on the hammer, the ignition popped out. He placed the tools back in the bag and picked out a flathead screwdriver. He stuck it into the hole that used to hold the ignition. When he turned forcefully, the car roared to life. He put it in drive and took off with Vill following closely behind. They drove back to Queens, parked James's Acura RL, then headed to Manhattan in the Maxima. They pulled around the corner from the jewelry store and parked at the other end of the block.

"You ready?" asked James.

"Hell, yeah, my man!"

James looked at Vill's hands and saw that they were shaking badly.

"Leave your gun here and go down to the store and get a papaya juice."

"For what?"

"Just do the shit!" James replied, frustrated with Vill's questioning his orders.

Vill exited the car and walked down the street. Ten minutes later he returned with the drink.

"Here's your drink."

"Nah, that shit is for you to drink."

"What for, I'm not thirsty, and I don't like papaya," said Vill.

"It's not for your thirst, it's for your nervousness. It'll help calm you down."

"Man, I'm not nervous."

"Just drink the fucking juice or we're not going anywhere."

Without another word, Vill opened the juice and drank it all.

"Okay, can we go now?"

"No, we'll wait until it flows into your body." James waited for about ten minutes before saying, "Let's go."

They tucked their guns into their waistbands before exiting the car. They walked up the street and turned the corner. Each carried a huge duffel bag in his hand. James began to put on his gloves, moving the bag from one hand to another. Seeing this, Vill did the same.

"Now listen good; I want you to handle the bitch. I'll take care of the nigga."

One store down from the jewelry store, they began pulling on their masks, stopping to allow a lady to pass them by. Once she was at a good distance, James warned Vill, "We're going in there to get the money, not catch a body."

"Nigga, I got you."

"This is it, let's go!"

Once they got to the door, they pulled their masks completely over their faces and entered promptly. Once inside, they brandished their guns. Both the man and lady froze in terror.

"Don't fucking move!" James shouted at them. He quickly made his way behind the viewing case and told the man, "Lay the fuck on the floor!"

"Get down on the floor, bitch! I'll blow off your head."

Both store clerks dropped to the floor quickly. The man began to shake uncontrollably as the lady began to cry, "Oh my God," over and over. James pulled out duct tape and bound their hands and feet. He then put a paper bag over their heads so they couldn't see.

"Quick, look around for any cameras."

As Vill went to look for any cameras in the store, James knelt down next to the man and asked, "Is there any hidden cameras in this store?"

"Th-th-there's none in here," he stuttered.

"If I find any cameras in here, I'm not going to kill you, but you will live to regret lying to me for the rest of your fucking life."

James then moved on to the lady. "Bitch, are there any cameras in here?"

"Oh my God, no," she cried out.

"I'll do your ass worse than him if you're lying to me."

She said nothing, but continued to cry.

James and Vill opened the jewelry cases and began to empty them out into the bags. Once they were done, James turned to the man. "What's the damn combination to the safe?"

"Twenty-two, fifty-eight, eleven."

With the combination, the safe was open in seconds.

"What's that fucking beeping?" Vill shouted.

The beeping continued without pause.

"I don't know what that shit is, but we been here too long," James replied.

With two sweeps of his hands, James emptied both shelves of the safe of all its contents, which was more cash and the very expensive jewelry.

"Come on, we out!"

James and Vill exited the store and calmly walked around the corner and down the block to the car. They opened the trunk and placed the bags inside.

"Your gun, mask, and gloves, too," James instructed Vill.

They then ripped off their warm-up suits and put them in the trunk as well. They were now dressed in slacks and button-downs. After closing the trunk, they walked down the block, made a right turn, and continued down the street.

Police cars began to fly by them heading in the direction of the jewelry store. They looked back and noticed that a number of squad cars had pulled up to the entry side of the bridge and blocked it. Others were blocking the streets and stopping traffic. James and Vill walked until they got to the movie theater, where they paid for two tickets and went in to watch a movie.

They stayed in the movie theater for the next seven hours. Meanwhile, the cops had set up checkpoints spanning a twenty-block radius. By the time the two exited the theater, the cops were packed up and long gone. The two walked back to find the Maxima exactly where they had left it.

"Hop in, my man, we're out."

Within minutes they were on their way over the Fifty-ninth Street bridge back to Queens.

"My nigga, that was a perfect plan, dawg. We are fucking paid!" Vill said with excitement. He then rolled the window down and screamed outside, "Woooooooo!"

"Yo, chill the fuck out with all that noise you making. What you trying to do? Bring attention to us?"

"My bad, my nigga. I'm just happy as a faggot with a bag of dicks right now."

"Well, just be cool."

"I ain't never had this kind of money before. I told you, didn't I? I told you that the shit was going to be easy."

"Yeah, you was right."

"Now a nigga could really get his shine on. I'ma be shitting on these bitches this year."

Vill continued to rant on about their success as James sat and listened quietly. Eventually, he decided to say something about the way Vill was carrying on.

"Vill, you know you can't just be going around rambling on about this shit. You can't start spending money like you crazy. People going to start putting one and one together if you do some shit like that."

"Come on Paw, what, you think a nigga stupid or something? I know how to do my thing, dog."

"Yo, I'm just reminding you."

"You ain't got to worry about anything getting back to you, so just be easy."

"Yeah, 'cause I don't need no fucking heat, man."

"I'm gonna do it like I'm doing it for TV! That don't mean I'ma be doing some dumb shit, so stop sweating."

James sat quietly for the rest of the ride to Queens. He was in deep thought. Finally he asked, "So where you want to split this shit up?"

"I don't care, anywhere is fine with me."

"So let's go to my place then."

James had parked his car on a deserted block. They pulled up behind it, got out, and transferred the bags from the trunk of the Maxima to James's car's trunk. Just as they were about to close the trunk James said, "Shit, I forgot the bag on the backseat of the Max. Snatch it for me."

Vill turned and went to the car and opened the door. He reached in for the bag of tools. As he began to back out, he felt the nozzle of something resting on the back of his head.

Bang! Bang!

The sound of the gunshots echoed, shattering the silence of the night. Vill's lifeless body fell forward onto the seat after James shot him twice in the back of his head. James then grabbed his bag and walked back to his car, got in, and drove away. He could not take the risk of allowing Vill's flashy stupidity to catch up with him.

EIGHT

Banit was sent to Rikers Island pending his court hearing and possible trial. He was charged with second-degree murder and a slew of armed robberies. He didn't hire a lawyer; instead, he used a court-appointed one. He felt getting a real lawyer would be a waste of money. He was well aware that if he was convicted, he would spend the rest of his life behind bars. He was upset at himself for allowing Cloud to come in and play him like a damn fool. *That motherfucker even killed my cousin. I got to get his ass back.*

Banit couldn't help thinking that because of his mistakes his cousin was dead. Ozzi's mother was now without a son and his son without a father. All this on account of him. He was doomed with all these charges against him. Even with the best plea-agreement lawyer, he would still be in jail for a long time. One option would be to help in the capture and conviction of the others. The problem was, he was at fault for all that had gone wrong. With that in mind, he was not about to make life miserable for everyone else on the account of his fuckup. It was better to go out with his nuts in his hands and not on the table. Snitching was out of the question.

Banit began to contemplate escaping during his many trips back and forth to court. He paid close attention to every detail, trying to find an open seam he could slip through. Security was too tight. He realized that even if he made it out of the building, getting off the island would be a more difficult feat. He needed help.

Ozzi's mother and Ignis, the mother of his son, visited Banit weekly. They were also present at his court hearing as a show of support. His plan was to tell his aunt and Ignis where his money was stashed once his case was complete and he was sentenced. He figured it was the least he could do for them.

MIAMI HAD A LARGE JAMAICAN population, which made Cat feel comfortable and right at home. There were also a lot of rich people there who had become rich by way of illegal activities. He began to mingle among them, carefully. He knew that he had to be extra careful because any of them could be under investigation, which could lead the cops to Cat. He was no fool. He was busy trying to leave the country without taking the risk of going through an airport. Everything was still too fresh, so he had no choice but to lie low for a while. In the meantime, he figured that he should start working on getting new identification.

He spent his nights visiting clubs, hoping to meet someone who could help him with establishing a new identity, and met a fellow Jamaican named Gamble. After running into each other on several occasions at various clubs, they began to seriously talk over drinks. Gamble then invited Cat to a barbecue at his home in the South Beach section of Miami.

The house was an immaculate mansion Gamble was renting. When Cat arrived, not only was he impressed with the home, but he was surprised to see the people in attendance. The place was filled with models, photographers, athletes, wealthy businessmen, and other obviously well-paid people. Fewer than seven blacks were at the barbecue, only a couple of them Jamaican. Cat was more curious than ever as to what exactly Gamble did for a living.

After moving around the party a bit, Cat ventured into what seemed to be the powder room. Enough cocaine and weed were there to supply a hot city block in the East New York section of Brooklyn. This amount of drugs could get someone a long time in prison if the cops were to run up in here. Cat began to think Gamble was a drug dealer, but he wasn't sure at what level.

He discovered later that Gamble was a club owner and one of the biggest party promoters in South Beach. His name was synonymous with the hottest parties. However, after a series of suspicious fires at several of his clubs, his license was suspended pending an investigation. He began throwing his parties in mansions that he rented. Cat found out Gamble wasn't providing the drugs for these parties. It was Bull. He was often seen with Gamble. Cat knew he had to be careful with how he dealt with these two because anything as big as what they were doing was sure to draw a lot of attention.

Cat's gut was telling him that he should leave this party, but he was too intrigued by Gamble's lifestyle, not to mention the party was nice. As the night came to a close, Cat and Gamble found themselves by the pool talking about the night.

"So how you like di party?"

"Me enjoy meself; big tings a gwan."

"Me glad for hear dat."

There was some silence as Cat contemplated how to approach Gamble.

"From yard mon to yard mon, it's not too hard to figure out how you do your thing."

"What you mean?" Gamble asked.

"Well, the whole atmosphere you provide here."

Gamble paused in silence for thought, then said, "Do you know why I invited you here tonight?"

"No, but tell me."

"Well, when me first meet you, there was something about you that me couldn't quite put me fingers on, but me know whatever it is, it would lead to me and you doing some big things together."

Cat held his head down and smiled. Gamble had him figured out all the while.

"You might be right, but right now I'm kinda hot. I have to lay low for a while, till things cool off. Then, maybe me and you can talk about some business."

"That's cool, my yute, but what you going to do in the meantime?"

"Well, right now I have a problem I have to fix first."

"What's that?"

"I need some new ID quick and fast. I can't move around like I want to."

"That's it?"

"That's it, brethren."

"My yute, that's no problem at all. Just give me a couple of days, and I'll have you hooked up."

Three days after the party, Cat called Gamble to see if he was ready or able to set him up with new identification.

"Brethren, everything is set for you. All you need for do is go to DMV and look for a girl name Cynthia. She should be at booth number four. She will be expecting you."

"Much thanks, brethren."

"Easy, just go get it. We talk later."

When his taxi pulled up at the Department of Motor Vehicles, Cat stepped out and walked inside. He looked around for booth number four, which was on his far left. Only one lady was in line, and Cat stood behind her. When the lady was done and walked away, Cat stepped forward. He read the clerk's nameplate as he approached her booth. Her eyes were still focused on the papers on her desk.

"Excuse me, uh, Cynthia?"

She looked up at Cat. It was as though both of them became lost in each other's stare. She swept her long, jet-black hair away from her face, revealing cocoa-colored skin, bright brown eyes, and a perfectly structured face. Not the type of look that one would expect to find sitting behind a desk. She should have been on the runway working top fashion shows. Cat was caught in a trance.

"Yes, how can I help you?" she said, revealing perfectly aligned, pearly white teeth.

Cat was still caught in his trance. Finally he was able to say, "Ahmm, my name is Tony, I was told that you would be expecting me."

"Oh, right, right. How are you? I almost forgot."

"I'm fine, thank you."

She stood up and began filing papers away in folders. "Give me a second, I'll be right with you."

"Take all the time you need."

Later that day Cat called Gamble and thanked him for hooking up his new license. It was free of charge. Cynthia told him that he would be getting a new Social Security card, then he would move on to get his passport.

"That sounds good," Gamble said. "What you say we get together and have a couple of drinks?"

Later that night they met at a bar called Panthers. Over drinks, Gamble told Cat about his club-owning days, and of his scam of burning them down to collect the insurance money. He let Cat know that he was in with the who's who crowd in Miami.

"When I throw a party, everybody that's somebody will come out to play."

Cat in turn told Gamble what he was about. He was careful not to give him specifics, but Gamble got the point. The two men decided that they could work together. As the conversation came to a close, Cat figured it would be a good time to ask about Cynthia.

"So you like my cousin, huh?"

"I didn't know that was your cousin." Cat felt a little embarrassed asking Gamble about a family member. He didn't want Gamble to take things the wrong way. "I ain't trying to be disrespectful or anything like that."

"Man, don't sweat that. It ain't nothing."

Cat relaxed, realizing that Gamble didn't mind him being interested in his cousin. "In that case, make that a big interest in your cousin."

Gamble laughed at Cat's response. "Well, I'll see what I can do to plug you in with her."

That was exactly what Cat wanted to hear.

"I'm also having another party this weekend. You should stop by. Who knows, your dream girl might show up."

BANIT WAS NOW WELL INTO the court proceedings and still plotting his escape. He befriended a young Jamaican correctional officer that worked in the yard. He figured that would be his best chance if he was to try an escape. He was counting on the officer's being not only young, but also Jamaican. Being a fellow countryman, it was easy to engage him in delicate conversation. After about ten months, the prosecution was pushing for trial. Banit kept telling his lawyer to postpone his court date for as long as possible. Banit called Ignis and told her that it was important that she visit him soon.

She came a few days later. On the visit with her, he told her, "There's no way I am going to beat this thing. Plus, I don't think I can live the rest of my life in prison."

"Oooo, Banit, I feel so bad."

"Listen, I'm going to take my chances and try to escape, because either way I'm fucked."

"What?" she almost screamed out.

"Ignis, I need your help."

"Banit, I have a son." Her voice was shaking. "I can't afford to get caught up in something that will get me locked up."

"I know and understand that."

"I am all he got out there, with his father gone."

"Don't worry about that. I wouldn't let nothing happen to you or your son. Your role in this will be very limited."

He told her about the money he had stashed away, and that all he needed her to do was to get it so he could use it to entice the officer into helping him. He told her that she would keep a million for herself, and a million would go to the officer. He would keep the remaining million for himself to run with. Maybe he could get over to Mexico or work his way to another country.

After hearing him out, Ignis figured that it was the least she could do for him. She could also use the money he was giving her. The plan was for her to approach the officer after he got off work and solicit his help. If she could get him to agree to help Banit, he would get half the money up front and the rest after Banit escaped.

The judge ordered Banit's lawyer to get ready for trial, but Banit needed more time. He fired his court-appointed lawyer and hired a private one. This would buy him some more time while the new lawyer familiarized himself with the case and devised a strategy for trial. Banit needed this time to get more familiar with the officer before Ignis approached him with the idea of helping Banit escape. He gave the officer's badge number along with his name, description, and the type of car he drove to Ignis.

A HALF HOUR BEFORE THE shift change, Ignis pulled up and parked at the corner of the street leading onto the bridge that connected Queens to Rikers Island. She watched as all the cars came over the bridge leaving the island, trying to see the officer she needed to approach. It didn't take long for her to spot him in the red Dodge Stratus. She waited for him to pass her car and followed him all the way to Coney Island in Brooklyn. He turned onto a block, drove up to the curb, and parked. As he exited the car, she pulled up next to him. He turned and looked as she rolled the passenger window down.

"Michael Brown?"

He leaned over to look into her car. "And who want to know?"

"Hello, my name is Tia. Do you mind if I take a minute of your time to talk?"

"As long as I'm not in any danger, you could take as much of my time as you want, sexy."

"No, no danger here whatsoever."

"Then in that case, let's start talking."

She pressed the automatic button and unlocked the door. He opened it and started to get in. He paused as if he began to have second thoughts, then seemed to change his mind and entered, closing the door.

"What did you say you wanted?"

"I didn't say what I wanted yet. Do you mind if we circle the block?"

"Go right ahead."

She drove off to the next corner. As she turned the block, she said, "I'm a close friend of Banit."

With Banit's name spoken, Brown turned and looked at her with caution. "What's all this about?"

Ignis took her time, knowing that she had to choose her words wisely. She didn't know which way to come out and say what needed to be said. "Banit needs your help."

"What do you mean, he needs my help? Needs my help for what?"

She felt the need to swallow, knowing that if she failed, Banit was surely doomed to prison for the rest of his life. He was depending on her to come through for him. She had to make this happen for Banit. "He needs your help in order to escape," she said as she drove around the next corner.

Michael's eyes narrowed. He couldn't believe what she just said to him. He thought she was about to ask him to bring Banit drugs of some sort. He would never have guessed that this was what she planned to ask him.

"Are you fucking serious?"

"Yes, I am."

"No, you can't be serious. This got to be a joke or something," he said, paying close attention to her face to get a sense if she was joking.

She stopped the car abruptly. "I am not joking," she said, looking directly into his eyes.

That scared him. He closed his eyes and

shook his head. "Lady, you are fucking crazy. Don't you know that I could get your ass arrested? Would you please drop me off back where you picked me up?"

She began to think she was losing him. "Please, just wait a minute, just hear me out."

"There's nothing to hear. I've heard all that I am prepared to hear. Plus I'm not ready to be in there with your boy. That is exactly what will happen if I try some shit like that. I have a family. There is no way I could be a part of some shit like that. No way whatsoever!"

Ignis began driving again.

Brown paused for a moment, then began shaking his head again. "I can't believe the fucking nerves of that guy. You just can't be nice to a fucking crook without them taking shit the wrong way. What the fuck he think this is!"

Ignis realized that she wasn't doing a good job of convincing Brown. She needed to turn the table someway, somehow, and fast. "I don't mean to offend you, but it's just that he thought you was someone that he could trust. You know, being Jamaican and all."

She pulled the car in front of his house and parked to drop him off.

"Look, Tia, I'm truly sorry that I can't help you, but what you are asking just isn't possible. You are crazy for trying something like this.

When I see that fucker tomorrow, he's in real trouble for trying to play me like this."

Brown opened the door and began to step out of the car. Just as he placed his right foot outside on the ground, she tapped his arm. "There's a million dollars in it for you, if you help."

That stopped him dead in his tracks. He turned and looked back at her to see if she still had a serious look on her face. "A mill-ion fucking dollars?" he asked slowly.

"That's exactly what I said."

He took a deep breath, allowing her words to sink in, as he placed his foot back into the car. At rapid speed images flashed across Michael's mind of what a million dollars could do for his family. They could move out of public housing, put his kids in private school, and finally go on a vacation for the first time in his life. "Let's take another spin around the block."

JAMES FLEW TO ATLANTA TO visit his uncle Prince. He figured that Prince was probably low on cash and could use some. It would be nice to see his grandmother, too. He hadn't seen her in three years.

When he arrived at the house, Prince was more than ecstatic to see him. They went out to the back porch to sit and catch up on things. As they spoke, James unzipped the bag he'd brought with him, pulled out a pouch, and passed it to Prince.

"What's this?" he asked as he caught the bag.

"Just open it, my man."

Prince quickly unzipped the pouch. "Oh, shit!" he screamed out loud, then reached inside and pulled out a handful of jewelry.

"My yute, where did you get all this shit from?"

"A little jux me come across a couple months ago."

"Damn! I see you still doing your thing."

"Me figure you might be low on funds by now."

Prince smiled at his nephew. He was glad that he had him as family. "You just in time because me on me last right now."

"Well, that should hold you down for a while. But let me tell you, I had to lick off a buoy head for dat." James told him about the jux, and how he pulled it off.

Then they talked about the crew and all that went down. They had no idea where everybody else was hiding out or anything else.

JAMES SPENT SEVEN DAYS IN Atlanta before flying back to New York. On his second day back home, he went to his old neighborhood to see what was going on. He wanted to know what was being said about what happened to Vill. He pulled up on his old block, where he used to hang out and hustle. The block was still as he left it, filled with run-down buildings and busy with people milling about. Underneath one lamppost was a group of stickup kids, their hoodies worn low to conceal their faces. Above them, draped over the streetlight cord by their shoestrings, were the sneakers of the six kids they had killed. Down the block were other groups of young men that were known as hand-to-hand drug dealers. Junkies would come up and quickly one of the young men would take their money and pull drugs from their hidden stash and pass them on. The transactions were performed so quickly that their actions were mostly unnoticed to the untrained eye. James could have run up on them and taken their money, but he knew they would have no more than a grand, so it wasn't worth his time.

The regular crowd was doing the same old thing of sitting on the hoods of cars talking junk, or rolling dice in the alleyway. This was not a way of life that James missed, and if it were up to him, he would move all of his friends out of the neighborhood. James double-parked and hopped out to greet his old buddies.

"Kaizer, Ant, what the fuck is up?"

"What's up, my nigga? You hardly come

around here anymore. You must be doing some big things," said Ant.

"Well, you know, I'm trying to keep my head above water, that's all."

"It looks like your whole body is floating to me," Kaizer shot back, noticing James's fly gear.

"Fuck all that, let's burn this spliff and get right." They smoked together and joked around until the weed was completely gone.

"Listen, I just came through to check my niggas. I have some things to take care of, so I gotta be out," James said, getting ready to leave.

He said his good-byes and told them both that he would be returning to see them soon. "I will have a little something for you."

He walked to his car, got in, and started it. Just as he was about to take his foot off the brakes, he heard what he thought was a gunshot. Another shot rang out, and another, and another. His passenger window was shattered. He felt numbness all over his body. He slumped over the passenger seat and covered his head for protection. Suddenly everything went black. The pressure of his foot came off the brake and his car began to roll into the intersection. It stopped when it collided with another car.

FOUR MONTHS LATER, JAMES REGAINED consciousness in the hospital. Eight shots were fired into his car. Luckily, only four hit him, two in his back, one in his shoulder, and one in his left side. It was the collision in the intersection that sent him into the coma. When he awoke, he didn't remember anything that happened the day of the shooting. His girlfriend, Symone, told him. His mother, sister, and brother all visited him throughout his stay in the hospital. Feeling the warmth and love from his family and Symone made James seriously contemplate changing his way of life. He began to think that he should try the straight and narrow. He had enough money to live comfortably. The question was, what would he do with his life? What kind of job would satisfy him?

Prince received word of the shooting and accident and came to visit James while he was still in the coma. Symone told Prince that the word on the streets was that Antwan, Vill's brother, had tried to kill James.

PRINCE STAKED OUT ANTWAN'S BUILDING for almost a month until one night while waiting in his car, he spotted a figure in a baseball cap and hood coming out of the building. He could not make out the face, but he was almost certain that it was him. He just had that feeling.

Prince watched as the person walked up the block. When he got far enough, Prince pulled out of his parking space and followed slowly in the distance. Prince kept his eyes on the person as he walked into a bodega. Five minutes later he came out and turned in the opposite direction, heading back to the building. Prince quickly made a U-turn and went on ahead of him. He pulled his car back around the building, parked, and went inside. The stairwell gave him a direct view of the elevator so he hid there, waiting.

The guy walked into the building, approached the elevator, and pressed the button. Prince could see him clearly now. Yes, it was definitely Antwan. Prince waited until the elevator door opened and Antwan got in. Running from the stairwell, he caught the elevator door just before it closed. He got in and held his head down so Antwan couldn't see his face. When he raised his head, Antwan recognized him immediately. All the color drained from Antwan's face. He was caught off guard, caught slipping. He felt nothing other than terror looking at the Beretta 93-R in Prince's hand pointed directly at his stomach.

"Hold this for James" was all Prince said as he pumped three shots into Antwan's midsection. He fired four more shots into Antwan's face so he couldn't have an open-coffin wake. Prince walked out of the elevator and exited the building. He wiped the gun down, dropped it into the sewer drain, got into his car, and headed back to Atlanta.

THE MANSION WAS PACKED WITH the usual people who frequented Gamble's parties. The pool was filled and the powder room had a steady rotation. Cat and Gamble were standing on the balcony, overlooking the pool.

"I don't know how you do what you do, but I can tell you that there is a lot of money here waiting to be taken. You see, most of these people won't even miss it." Gamble motioned toward a young Italian man standing by the pool talking to three ladies. "Like take that Finon over there, for example. His father is the head of a major cartel. He supplies at least a third of the Eastern Seaboard with heroin."

"Yeah?"

"That kid never have to work a day in his life. Not only that, his father is almost Teflon. The government will not touch him because he bankrolled almost half the Gulf War. At least that's what they say. He can give billions to any government project or even run for some political office, and that dude you're looking at is his son."

Gamble paused and looked over the crowd. "Those three brothers over there make millions in the drug trade. Lydia, who, by the way, I would love to fuck, made millions by ripping off pharmaceutical companies. That asshole over there in the black suit is the owner of the largest trucking company on the East Coast. Every year millions of dollars in merchandise goes missing. Can you believe that he has a huge fish tank with five million dollars in hundred-dollar bills all cut up in it?"

"You serious?" Cat asked, while rationalizing that to make it big in the world, to have money, one has to be involved in something illegal. He considered the Kennedys and how they got their money by selling alcohol during Prohibition. Going the straight-job route just did not seem to work.

"Yes, he has it in his house. No bullshitting. These people have nothing better to do with their money."

"But all these people know you and seem to like, if not love, you."

"Man, they all look at me as being below them, even though I'm the one they come to for their cherry high. I don't give a fuck about them either. I just want some of their money."

"I see. I would love to have some of their money, too."

There was a pause as Gamble looked into Cat's eyes as if trying to read him. Gamble then waved his right hand from his left shoulder back to his right. "You have every victim you will ever need right in here. I could open their doors to you, Cat. I think you're the man for the job."

"Is that so?" was all Cat could say in response to all that Gamble had said. He wasn't sure if he should trust Gamble so quickly. On the other hand, Gamble would lose just as much if he crossed Cat. Matter of fact, all these people knew Gamble, not him.

"Yes, that is." Gamble turned to look at Cat and saw Cynthia walking toward them over Cat's shoulder. "There's my favorite cousin."

Cat turned around to see her walking toward them, dressed in a red dress and pumps to match. Once again he was caught in a trance, as if this were the first time he had ever laid eyes on her. As she approached them, for the first time ever the thought of settling down and getting married crossed Cat's mind. Cynthia walked over to Gamble and embraced him.

"I have someone that I want you to meet," he said. "In fact, I believe the two of you already met."

After reintroducing the both of them, Gamble began to walk away. "Let me leave the two of you alone to talk and hopefully get to know each other better."

Cat was at a loss for words. He knew that

she would be coming to the party, so he had spent many hours thinking of what he would say to her. Now here she was, standing before him, and he could find no words.

At last she bailed him out. "So here we meet again."

"Yes." He had to laugh. "Please forgive me, I'm not usually at a loss for words. It is my pleasure to meet you again."

She looked at him for a brief moment. "You seem to be a gentleman, so it leads me to wonder why a person like you would be in need of new identification?"

She had caught him off guard. He didn't expect her to ask such a direct question. Not knowing what to say, he simply held his head down and smiled.

"I hope you're not some kind of outlaw . . . maybe a mass murderer or something," she said in a joking manner.

"No, I'm nothing like that. I just got into a little trouble and need to lay low for a while. At least until things blow over. It's nothing you need to worry yourself about. You're safe with me."

"I hope so. My mother always told me to stay away from bad guys, especially the ones that need new ID. So are you enjoying yourself?"

"If I wasn't before, I am now." He began to feel good, especially when they made a date.

BANIT'S PLANS TO ESCAPE WERE on their way. Ignis had retrieved the money from where Banit had hid it. She delivered the first payment of $500,000 to Michael as planned. The other half was due after Banit escaped. After the transaction, she informed Michael that their deal was recorded on tape. She explained to him that it was simply insurance for him to keep his side of the bargain. She assured him that he would receive the only copy of the tape along with his final payment after Banit had escaped.

Michael set his plans in motion. He had to enlist the help of another officer he trusted because whenever a prisoner is transported, he or she must have two officers as escorts. It would be almost impossible for Michael to slip Banit by the other officer without being noticed.

The plan was to allow Banit to escape during the court run. Michael kept a close watch on the upcoming court schedule. He needed to execute his plan on a day that the court had a high volume of court appearances. When he saw a day that would work, he informed Banit, who in turn called his lawyer and asked him to request that date from the judge. The judge granted the court date, and Michael and his partner put their bid in to work the court runs scheduled for that day. They would be transporting twenty-two prisoners, the maximum allowed to be transported by two officers.

Banit was awake by 4 a.m. that morning. He showered and dressed. He made sure to eat some instant oatmeal, not knowing when he might be able to eat again. He then sat down in the open day room watching the news while he waited for his name to be called for court.

His name was the last to be called by the officer. "Richard Williams, to the court pen," the officer shouted.

Banit stood up and began to hop along on his right foot, crutches under his arms. The day before, while in the yard, he faked an ankle injury while playing basketball. Michael told him to do this so he'd have a medical pass. With the pass, he would be the last man placed on the bus, and the last man off the bus. It also meant he'd be cuffed and chained alone. Everything was going according to plan.

The bus was finally on its way across the Rikers Island bridge, and Banit was on it. Twenty minutes later, the bus pulled into the driveway of the Queens Criminal Court on Queens Boulevard in the Kew Gardens section of Queens. There, the prisoners were ordered to exit the bus and enter the court building to be processed.

The drive path at the courthouse had no gates or fences surrounding it. It was simply a driveway at the side of the building where the bus pulled up to the door and prisoners were let off. Banit was the last to get off the bus. He was instructed by Michael to walk slowly to get a good distance from the other prisoners. That way none of them would see him when he walked away.

Banit stepped off the bus, made a right turn, and began walking up the driveway away from the building. As he walked, he pulled a handcuff key that Michael had given him out of his pocket and unlocked his handcuffs. Once he got onto the sidewalk of the street, he hailed a taxi and was off to his newfound freedom.

Michael paid his partner $250,000 out of the $500,000 he received from Tia. Once Ignis saw on the nightly news that Banit had escaped without incident, she called Michael and gave him the number to the post office box where he would find the rest of his money along with the recording. She also told him that he would find the key to the box under the front passenger floor mat of his car.

The national news covered Banit's escape for two weeks. Cat, Prince, and James caught it all on the news. Prince and James were both surprised to hear that Banit was incarcerated, but happy to hear that he had escaped. They began to wonder if Cat was locked up as well. As for Cat, he knew Prince and James were free because he was able to keep tabs on everyone, except Cloud. He was especially proud of Banit's ability to put an escape plan together. Though he was on the run, he was free like the rest of them.

NINE

James was out of the hospital and working hard on his recovery and rehabilitation. With Symone's assistance, he quickly regained most of his weight and strength. He was glad to be alive. As soon as he was released from the hospital, he bought himself a new BMW, wanting nothing to do with the Acura he was shot in. The car listed for $67,000, but fully loaded it would cost James about $80,000. He sold five rings from his collection and was off to the car dealer.

Two weeks later he and Symone went to pick it up. He walked into the showroom, and there was his gold BMW 7 Series, sitting on twenty-inch rims gleaming under the lights of the showroom.

"Man, that's beautiful, ain't it?" he said to Symone.

"It sure is," she replied, equally as happy as he was.

The dealer opened the door and handed him the keys. James hopped into the driver's seat, and Symone quickly made her way to the passenger seat. He lifted his head and inhaled the scent of new leather. Symone did the same.

"Baby girl, look at all this bird-eye maple. This is a custom system you see sitting in the console." He wrapped his hands around the steering wheel. "This is definitely what I'm talking about, this is a real car."

"Boo, this is the bomb!" said Symone while running her hands across the maple finish.

"This bad boy can rocket from zero to sixty in just five seconds, pumping out a whopping three hundred and two horsepower that will snap your head back to that special handwoven leather headrest," said the salesman. "It has a seven-speed transmission, Airmatic DC air suspension, luxury dual climate control. This baby combines coupe elegance with a sedan's practicality. Simply put, the E-Class is the finest car in its class. It is unmatched, period."

James drove off the showroom lot and headed for the Diamond District in Manhattan. They pulled up and parked in front of Tiffany's. Symone looked a bit puzzled.

"He's probably picking up some jewelry for himself," she said, barely audible.

James opened the door and showed her in. She never knew the store was so large, with all sorts of exotic jewelry and artwork. They walked to the end of the display counter where one of the representatives recognized James.

"Sir, you are right on time. Your order came in just one hour ago. Just give me one minute and I will be right back with it." The store clerk was off to the back.

James leaned against the counter, looked at Symone, and smiled.

"What are you smiling at me like that for?" She didn't know what to make of all that was going on. What she did know is that it wasn't looking like anything she was hoping for. The hair standing on her neck when they'd first walked in was now relaxed. She only looked forward to seeing what he had ordered.

Symone began to notice that more and more people who seemed to be employees of the store were slowly gathering, surrounding them. This made her feel a bit crowded. They seemed to be watching them, but trying not to be noticed. They were now awfully close to them. She wondered if James saw what was happening. She looked at him and saw that he had no clue as to what was going on around them.

The salesman finally returned, holding a small box in both his hands as if its contents would break with one tremble. Suddenly, all the employees surrounded them. Symone had a strong urge to take off running. What kept her from doing just that was James standing there staring and smiling at her. The salesman handed the box to James. Her head began to spin. She felt as though she would pass out. The circle around them got tighter. She couldn't catch her breath. No, she was in fact holding her breath. James then turned the box around in his hands so that the front was facing her. He began to open it slowly. She couldn't believe what she thought was happening was actually happening. Then in unison, all the employees shouted, "Symone, will you marry me?"

She could not believe her ears. Did she hear what she thought they just shouted? She looked down to see a huge princess-cut diamond, set in polished platinum, sparkling under the lights. She felt the need to scream, so she placed her hands over her mouth to prevent it.

"Oh my God, James. I can't believe this!"

"Believe it, baby girl."

Tears began to roll down her cheeks, and she became weak in the knees.

"I love you. I love you, James. Yes, yes, I will marry you," she cried as she jumped forward into his arms. The entire store erupted in cheers.

After his close call with death, James wanted to start a fresh life with Symone and leave his criminal ways behind him. To celebrate, they would fly to Hawaii, but first James wanted to stop off in Atlanta and see Prince. He wanted to thank him for handling Antwan. James and Symone flew down there two days later. His grandmother cooked a big meal for the four of them, and they sat and ate till they were full. After dinner, Symone and his grandmother showered and went to bed. James and Prince went out on the back porch to talk. They pulled up two summer chairs and sat down. James then went into his pocket and pulled out a bighead spliff and tossed it to Prince.

"Light that up, fam."

"Now, that's what I'm talkin' 'bout," Prince said as he caught it. He flipped open his Zippo to light it. Prince took a long pull on the spliff, inhaling the smoke, causing him to almost choke, but he held it. After he exhaled, he said, "That's some good bloodclaat herb, my yute." He slapped his tongue against his gums trying to get a taste of the weed.

"That's yard weed there," said James. "Me can taste it."

Prince took two more tokes, then passed the

herb to James. After James exhaled his first pull, he turned to Prince. "I want you to know that I'm feelin' you for takin' care of that nigga for me while I was down."

"Come on, Neph. You ain't gotta mention it. That's what family's for."

The two chatted all night until they both fell fast asleep outside in their chairs. The next morning, Symone found them in the same spot. "I know y'all didn't sleep there like that all night!"

They both jumped out their sleep at the sound of her voice. "You know we have a flight to catch in three hours?"

James tried to move, but his body was stiff and in pain from sleeping in such an awkward position all night. Within an hour, they were ready to go. An hour was all they needed to get to the airport, which was not too far away. James and Symone said their good-byes to his grandmother and were off.

Prince decided that he would drive them. As they came to a stop two corners from the house, suddenly a gray Audi pulled up alongside them. It beeped its horn and Prince rolled his window down. Prince's and James's faces reflected their surprise. It was Cat. They couldn't believe their eyes. They pulled over to greet him. Symone looked on from the back window as the three men embraced one another.

"Oh, shit! What's going on, man! I never thought that I would have seen you again alive and well," said Prince.

"I'm here, man, alive and well."

"How you find us?" asked James.

"Come on, man. It's me you talking to."

They laughed.

"That's true, you definitely right about that. So what brings you around?"

"I need some help. I'm down in Miami, the fucking place is just crawling with people waiting for us to take their money, but I need some serious help. I already have some big jobs lined up, and right now you two are the only ones that I can trust and depend on. Y'all know that Banit just escaped from prison and Ozzi is dead?"

Both James and Prince were surprised to hear that Ozzi was dead. They had no idea. James took Ozzi's death as confirmation that he needed to live a different life.

Prince shrugged his shoulders. "I don't care, you know I'm wit it!"

Cat and Prince slapped five and hugged each other.

"I'll talk to Symone and get back to you guys," said James tentatively.

Surprised by James's response, Cat and Prince looked at each other quizzically.

"I'll just wait out here for a while until she's

done chewing your head off," Prince said jokingly.

James walked back to the car and got into the backseat. Symone did not know who Cat was, but she could tell something was up and she didn't like it. James took a deep breath, looked her in the eyes, and told her the deal. He just knew that Symone would be against his risking his life again and that she would especially not want to postpone their trip to Hawaii and end up flying back to New York alone.

"How much money is your friend talking?" Symone asked after James explained the scenario.

James reached over and took her in his arms. "Look, Cat doesn't think small, but this is going to be risky."

"You ain't scared, are you?" Symone questioned with a daring look in her eyes.

"Naw, naw, baby, it ain't that," James said as he let go of Symone.

"Well, then, handle your business."

"That's the thing. I'm not sure I want this to be my business anymore," James said, dropping his head. "We have a nice car, a decent place to live, and some cash saved up. Do you really think this is necessary given everything that has happened?"

"Baby"—Symone moved closer to James—

"how about we make this the last time? I know you can do it and everything will be all right. I believe in you. Don't you want us to have the best of everything?"

"Just this last time, then. Since it means so much to you. When I look into your beautiful eyes, I can't say no. You know that."

Symone reached for James and they kissed long and passionately.

"I promise when I get back, I'll do whatever you want to do, wedding and all that. While I'm away, I want you to be a strong girl for daddy. Can you do that?"

Symone smiled. "Yes."

"Now I'ma go out and get this bread for the both of us, so just be easy and hold it down for me, you dig?"

"Yes," said Symone, dreaming about the jewels and clothing she would be able to buy and impress her friends with.

Banit picked up his share of the money that was left by Ignis in a run-down motel in Brooklyn. She rented the room two days before the escape and gave the keys to Michael, who in turn gave them to Banit. He picked the money up from a suitcase inside the closet, then left right away. He knew he couldn't stay in the city too long or he'd risk the police catching up to him.

First thing on his mind was to find Cat and the rest of the crew to warn them about Cloud.

From the motel, Banit took a livery cab to Yonkers, New York. He got out on First Street and rented a motel room close by for the night just to get his thoughts together. He was still high off the adrenaline rush from the escape. He couldn't believe he was a free man. He stopped at the vending machine and bought himself a sandwich, soda, and some candy bars. The room was small and cramped with a view of the side of the motel. That didn't matter to him. All he wanted was a good night's sleep to clear his head.

He awoke from a deep sleep at 3 p.m. the next day. His mind was definitely clearer. An idea had come to him in his sleep and he decided to get moving to put it into action. James was integral to the plan because Cloud had nothing to connect him to the rest of the crew, other than that he was present at The Lodge meetings. He and Cloud had never been on a jux together. Banit recognized that James wasn't in The Order that long before things fell apart.

Banit also knew that James was not yet apprehended, which meant that the police were not after him as hard as they were after Cat and Prince. Banit believed that James was still in the city and needed his help to take down Cloud. He had to get moving.

Banit wanted revenge on Cloud for ruining everything for him and his friends. That Cloud was able to play him for such a fool ate away at him hard. He spent every day in his cell thinking about revenge. Ozzi was dead. Banit wanted Cloud to pay with his life.

First thing Banit needed was a gun. He would also need clothes and a disguise. He remembered seeing a mall up the road when he was passing by in the cab. He got a few dollars out of the suitcase and left the room for the plaza. He entered one of the clothing stores and began to look through the racks of clothes. Roughly twenty minutes later, he was at the cash register paying for the things that he'd picked up. He had two pairs of jeans, two slacks, five shirts, some T-shirts, underwear, and socks. He then went next door to an all-purpose store and bought some cosmetics. He also picked up some hair dye, glue, hair weave, scissors, a needle, and a JanSport bag.

After returning to his motel room and putting his things away, he then went back out into the neighborhood surrounding the motel. He walked until he came upon what was obviously a high-traffic drug area. He approached one of the young men standing on the corner and asked him if he knew where he could get a gun. The young man asked him if he was a cop or something.

"No, me want ta shat a babylon boy," Banit responded.

The youngster was relaxed once he heard the Jamaican accent. "So what you looking for?"

"Maybe a .380 or something in that department."

"You got three hundred dollars?"

"You got a .380?"

"Follow me."

They walked a few blocks. When they got to a building, the kid told Banit to wait for him in the stairwell. Fifteen minutes later he was back with a Browning, double-action .380 and a box of bullets.

"The bullets is gonna cost you extra, if you want them."

"That's no problem."

After Banit paid for the gun and the bullets, the young man told him that if he ever needed anything else to come and see him.

Banit was set. Back at his motel room he went to work on his disguise. With the weave he made a hairpiece and a beard that he dyed gray. He got dressed and put on his makeup.

He left the motel, caught a cab to the Metro North train station, and got on the next train to New York City. At Penn Station, he rented two lockers and put his bags inside one of them. Then he headed for LeFrak City.

TEN

Cat, James, and Prince were back in Miami planning their next jux, scheduled to go down the next day. But Cat first wanted them to get some new identifications. A meeting was scheduled with Cynthia.

The target was Pecho, a Cuban-American who had made millions from the smuggling of Latin American immigrants into the United States. Families and friends would pay him hundreds of thousands of dollars to bring their loved ones to the United States. Somehow, he had a lot of connections with border patrols, who also took a cut of the payouts.

Sometimes Pecho would have the immigrants held in secret places while he negotiated more money from the family members to have them released. On occasion, he would demand sexual favors from the girls he smuggled across the borders, or from a family member he found attractive.

Pecho lived with his wife and sixteen-year-old daughter in a gated house in South Beach. Each neighbor lived about a block apart from the other. Three dogs were in the yard, so Cat and his crew cooked up a special beef-and-gravy treat for the dogs. Mixed in the gravy was chloral hydrate. They visited the house around 11 p.m. and threw the three plastic bags containing the beef and gravy over the fence. The large dose of chloral hydrate in the food knocked the dogs out within minutes.

By the time the crew returned at around 1:30 a.m., there were no dogs to hassle them. They entered the yard over the back fence. They checked all the ground-floor windows for any sign of movement. Through a second-floor window, they could see a television light on. They believed that this was the master bedroom. No alarm boxes were visible on the outside of the house. However, a security system was in place. This meant that the phone wire could not be cut. It would send a silent alarm to the security company or the police. If it was armed, the windows or doors could not be opened without tripping it. This was considered a minor problem.

Cat had developed some new techniques since the last time the crew was together. He brought a propane torch and a thermos filled with cold water. James kept his eyes peeled for any disruptions while Prince assisted Cat. The torch was lit. The trick was to put the torch to the glass on the window and heat it up. Once it got to a high enough temperature, they would throw the cold water from the thermos onto the windowpane. This would crack the glass all over without sending a strong enough vibration through the glass to trip the alarm. Having repeated this several times, Cat heated a small section on the bottom part of the windowpane and once again threw some cold water on it. This caused that section of the glass to shrink and separate from the rest of the cracked pieces. He then put a tiny suction cup on a piece of the glass and gently worked it loose. Once it was released, they worked the rest of the pieces out with their hands until enough glass was cleared to grant them ample space to slide through. The whole process took about fifteen minutes.

When they were finished, Cat was the first to climb through. James watched the front stairs while Prince and Cat searched the ground floor and the basement. All was clear downstairs. It was time to move upstairs to the bedrooms. Cat led the way with James behind on his left and

Prince in back on his right. One bedroom was on the right and one on the left, with the master bedroom straight ahead.

The door to the room on the right was wide-open. In the dark, a body was visible on the bed. Before she was able to shake off the sleep, Cat and James quickly gagged and bound the daughter by her hands and feet, while Prince looked out for any sign of alarm. Cat whispered to her that no harm would be done to her as long as she did as she was told.

"I'm going to ask you some questions and all I want you to do is nod your head yes or no, you got it?"

She nodded yes.

"Good. Now, is there anyone else in the house besides your parents?"

She shook her head no.

"Do your father have a gun in the house?"

She nodded yes.

"Do he sleep with it."

She shook her head no.

"Do he keep it locked away?"

She nodded yes.

"Okay, you're doing good."

They then took her into the hallway and laid her on the floor by her parents' bedroom door. Cat then held his hand up and counted to three with his fingers. At three they pushed the room door open and rushed in, jumping on the bed and overpowering the couple before they realized what was going on. Professional speed and accuracy came into play as they tied and gagged their victims. James then led the daughter into the room and laid her next to her mom. Prince began to search the room. Cat knelt down next to Pecho and rolled him over onto his back.

"I'm sure you know what my friend is looking for, so the easier you make this, the faster we will be out of your life."

Pecho was silent with a defiant look on his face.

"So you're not going to help us out, are you?"

Still no answer.

"You know you have a sexy wife here?" Cat reached over and put his hand on Pecho's wife's ass and began to rub it.

Pecho still did not respond.

Cat then raised her nightgown up to her waist. "I can bet she got some good Spanish-fly pussy up under here." He put his hand into her panties and began to move down the crack of her ass until his fingers were at the slit of her clit. "I bet she would love it. She's getting really wet down there, fella."

Still Pecho resisted and said nothing. Cat looked over at Prince, who was next to the daughter. Cat then reached over and turned the wife onto her back. "Your husband is a tough nut to crack."

He then propped her head up onto the pillow so she could get a clear view of Prince. He nodded his head, and with no hesitation Prince reached up under their daughter's nightgown. With one tug, he ripped her panties off and held them up in his hand. Her mother let out a muffled scream as she looked over at Pecho chanting muffled sounds at him. The girl began to cry for her mother.

"Oh, this is no game! My little friend is very eager!"

Prince then reached up under her gown and began to rub her pussy. Seeing that, her mother became hysterical and began to mumble as if she was trying to say something. Cat reached over and pulled the tape from her mouth.

"The back of the closet. It's at the back of the closet. The wall slides to the right. I believe that is what you're looking for."

James quickly moved the clothes out of the way and found the seam in the wall and slid it back. A wall safe with a combination was revealed. Cat looked at the lady again.

"Forty-five left three times, twenty right once, and nine left."

James hollered back, "Got it."

"Thank you for being such a good host," Cat said with a smile. The three of them had duffel bags on their backs. James and Cat tossed their bags to Prince and he began to fill them up.

An hour and ten minutes later they were all back at Cat's apartment laughing and congratulating one another.

"See, me tell you there was money down here, and easy money, too. Look how easy that was!"

They split the money down $600,000 apiece. The remaining $400,000 was set aside for Gamble. As they were splitting the jewelry, a ring caught James's eye. "Let me get that right there!"

He reached for the ring and began to look it over. A princess-cut, it had five and a half carats set in a rose-gold band.

"This should impress Symone," he said with a smile.

The next morning Cat met with Gamble to give him his share of the money.

"I knew you was the fucking man the minute I saw you," said Gamble, excited. "We are going to be fucking rich, rich I tell you, just keep fucking with me and we are going to be filthy rich." Gamble paused, savoring getting his share. "You want a drink?"

"Sure, why not."

They walked to the bar and Gamble went into the cooler for two beers.

"It would take me over a year of throwing parties to see this in profit. All it took you was one night. I'm loving this! I'm gonna be ready for you again in about a week. Me waiting for dis man for come back from Europe. In the meantime, I will give you the address and you can check the area out."

"That sounds like a plan."

They both took a few sips of their beers.

"So me hear that you and Cynthia have a date?"

"Oh, I forgot to tell you, this weekend we suppose to hook up."

Gamble laughed as he patted Cat on his shoulder. "That's me favorite cousin, so make sure you treat her right."

"You don't have to worry about nothing, my yute, she is safe, seen."

"All right, then enjoy yourselves."

THE WEEKEND FINALLY CAME. CAT and Cynthia were out on their date. Cat played the perfect gentleman. He was not pushy with anything. He let her pick where they ate mainly because he was not too familiar with the city as of yet. After dinner, they went for a walk on the beach and chatted for hours. Time seemed to slow down when Cat was with Cynthia. Being around her made him feel that money didn't matter. As they got to know each other and the chemistry between them continued to brew, he felt content. Later that night, he drove her home and left her with a kiss on the cheek and a hug, feeling her smile was all he needed to be happy. On his way back to his apartment, he whispered to himself, *Just one last jux.*

THE FOLLOWING WEEK THE CREW were ready for their next job. Cat had already checked the place out a few days earlier. Normally, it would be better to enter these houses when the owners weren't home. But things were different with these jux here in Miami. For one, the money was far greater, and this meant it would be tucked away in a safe of some sort. With a greater volume of money, the safe would take too much time and energy to try to open on the spot. Moreover, they had not mastered safecracking. They would have to take it down when the house was occupied, that way the occupants could open the safe.

The next target was Tommy, a Chinese heroin smuggler who had a wife and ten-year-old son. He did not live a lavish lifestyle in America, not having a mansion or an expensive house, but a regular two-story house in a relatively quiet neighborhood. He kept a low profile, yet did love partying with Gamble, who provided him with young, white hookers. He loved white girls—the one indulgence he had hidden away from his family.

Back in China, it was totally different. He lived it up in every conceivable way. He owned several mansions and mingled with all the aristocrats.

His Miami house was located in a working-class neighborhood, so by 11 p.m. everything was pretty quiet. The crew pulled up in a stolen BMW and parked two blocks behind the house. Some yards had dogs, but from mapping out the area days before, they had charted a clear course through the yards and over fences. They staked the house out until 3 a.m. before they began to work on it. The house did not have any security-company system that they could detect from outside. Chances were, this meant that it didn't have any at all. A security company would have a sign to ward off any potential burglars. The ground-floor windows had bars on them, but they were not cemented into the frame of the house. They were screwed into the outer wall and could easily be bypassed.

First thing they did was cut the phone wires to the house and the two houses next door. Then they placed a two-by-four between the bars and pried them apart slowly until the space was big enough for them to fit through. They struggled to wiggle their way through, but eventually they made it. Everything inside was quiet. As usual, they took up their positions. James took up watch by the steps that led upstairs, while Cat and Prince searched the rooms on the ground floor. All was clear. They made their move up the steps. The first room they came to was a bathroom, the next one was an empty bedroom. They quickly moved on to the next room, which was the master suite.

Tommy, his wife, and their son were all lying on the bed fast asleep with the son in the middle. Cat walked over and stood by Tommy. Prince went to the other side and stood over the wife, while James stood at the foot of the bed. Cat pointed his gun at Tommy's head, then tapped him on his forehead with it to wake him up. Tommy was startled and confused as he opened his eyes and saw these masked men surrounding him and his family.

"Shee, take it easy there, guy, not a sound now." Cat put his hand on Tommy's chest. His wife awoke at the sound. "Don't fucking move or I will blow your brains out."

James put his hand on her chest to hold her down. "Don't move."

They turned their prisoners onto their stomachs and began to bind them with duct tape. The boy woke up and the mother said something in Chinese to him. He lay back down on the bed and didn't move.

"English from now on!" said James.

"I only told him to lay down and be still," she replied.

"That's really good, I can see that everything is gonna go very smoothly."

After tying Tommy up, Cat sat him up on the bed. "Look, I'm sure you put it together as to why we are here, so let's not make this a long and tragic night. You understand?"

Cat tapped him once on the top of his head with the butt of his gun. Tommy nodded yes.

"So where's the money?" Cat asked.

"What money? What are you talking about? I don't have any money."

"Okay then, have it your way."

James immediately lifted Tommy's wife's nightgown and began to pull her panties off. Tommy sat there saying nothing, and his wife did not resist or show any signs of discomfort.

"Holy shit, that's a nice, fat, hairy pussy she got there! I bet she would be a good fuck!" said Cat.

"You making mistake, I have no money," Tommy yelled out with his Chinese accent.

Cat smacked him across the face with his

gun. Blood came running down his face. "You're lying, Tommy! You better tell me where the stash is or you and your family are dead!"

Still there was nothing from Tommy. Cat then motioned to Prince for the wire cutters. Prince went into his pouch and passed the tool to him. Cat then pulled Tommy's underwear off. "You ready to start talking?" Cat asked as he put the wire cutters to Tommy's dick.

"I don't have any money!" was all that Tommy angrily yelled.

Cat then told Prince to tape Tommy's mouth, which he did. Cat then put the cutters around the head of his dick and applied a bit of pressure. Tommy's eyes widened as he began to let out muffled screams.

"What? I can't hear you man. What you said? You ready to talk now?"

Cat reached up and peeled the tape off. Tommy huffed and puffed and kept repeating that he had no money. Cat reapplied the tape to Tommy's mouth and went back to putting even more pressure on his dick. The cutters cut into him and his cock began to bleed. Cat then took the tape off again and asked him if he was ready to tell him where the stash was. But still Tommy was not saying what they wanted to hear.

"This motherfucker got a high tolerance for pain," Cat said to James.

Prince started to search the home for the goods. As he walked out of the room, he heard what he thought was a squeak from a floorboard in the hallway. He stopped to listen. He heard nothing. He walked out of the room and started down the hallway back toward the steps. There was the squeak again. It came from a room that they had searched earlier, but found empty. Prince hugged the wall with his back. With not enough time to alert Cat and James, he got down low at the room's door and quickly peeked in. He saw a figure in the dark moving away from him, which meant that the person was not likely armed. He rushed in and tackled the person, surprised at how easily he overpowered the figure. Prince jumped on top and pointed his gun at the person.

"Don't fucking move!"

"Okay, okay, please don't hurt me."

"Shut the fuck up!"

Prince could not see the person well due to the darkness, but he soon realized that it was a female.

"Take it easy, just be still and you won't get hurt. Is there anyone else in here?"

"No."

"Get the hell up, bitch."

Prince took her into the master bedroom with everyone else.

"Look at what I found."

"Where did she come from?" asked Cat.

"She was hiding out in the front room."

"Damn, we're slipping," announced Cat.

Tommy looked disappointed when he saw them bring his wife's sister, Wing Yi, who was visiting from China, into the room.

"Listen here, you slanty-eyed fuck! I'll be in the bathroom with this pretty little young thing until you're ready to talk," said Prince as he grabbed Wing Yi by the hair and led her into the bathroom. Ever since Cat had told him and James about his first jux, Prince had often fantasized about a similar situation.

"I always wanted to fuck me a Chinese bitch. I hear y'all got the tightest pussy on the planet. Take your clothes off!"

She did not move.

"I said take your damn clothes off!" This time Prince pointed his gun at her.

With her head down, she slowly began to remove the shoulder straps of her nightgown, letting it fall to the ground. Prince immediately got a hard-on seeing the jet-black pubic hair sticking out from the side of her panties. She did not have much breast, but her nipples were the size of a pencil eraser. He then pointed to her underwear. "Take them off now!"

"Please don't do this."

"Shut up! Don't let me hear another word out of you, unless it's about where he's got that money stashed," Prince said.

She hesitated for a second, then complied. He then unbuckled his belt and dropped his pants to the floor. She stared in fright at the bulge in his underwear. She then looked up at him, but this time she had a different look in her eyes. Not the same nervous look as before.

"His son," she said.

"What you say?"

"His son."

"His son?" Prince repeated, confused. "What about his son, bitch?"

She took a deep breath and swallowed the saliva in her mouth. "You could torture me, my sister, or even him until the end of time, and he won't ever talk. But if you threaten his son, he will give you whatever you want on a platter."

Prince wished that she had not given him this information so soon, he wanted to play with her a bit more. Prince pulled up his pants, buckled his belt, and reached for the door.

"You come back?" asked Wing Yi.

Prince turned to look at her to see if she was serious. She had that look on her face again. He smiled and she smiled back. He closed the door behind him and went into the bedroom to give Cat the information about threatening the son.

When Cat heard this, he smacked himself on the forehead. "Damn, that's right, how the fuck I forget something like that?"

"What's that?" asked James.

"It's Chinese tradition that they value the male baby over the girl. That is why almost all Chinese kidnapping is of a male and never a female. They will pay the ransom on the male but leave the female to her fate."

Prince went back to the bathroom while James went to work on the son. When he got back to the bathroom and opened the door, he was surprised to see Wing Yi standing fully naked in front of him. He quickly went in and closed the door behind him, pulling his pants and underwear down to his ankles. Wing Yi gasped at the size of his dick. He knew that if what she told him was true, Cat and James would have everything wrapped up in no time, so he didn't have much time to waste. He put his hand on top of her head and slowly pushed her to her knees. She was now staring at his dick, eyes wide-open.

"Ever seen one this size?" he asked proudly.

She blushed and cracked a smile as she shook her head no.

"Go ahead, touch it."

With sort of a girlish and giddy smile she slowly reached her hand out and took ahold of it. As her warm hand wrapped around it, his dick became flushed with blood, rock hard in her hand. He moved closer to her face while at the same time bringing her head closer to him.

"Open your mouth and suck it."

She complied, and he slowly guided himself into her mouth. He let out a sigh and tilted his head back as the warm wetness of her mouth and tongue surrounded his manhood. He looked south as she began to take it in and out of her mouth. She could hardly handle the size as she struggled not to gag. He pulled his dick out and began to rub the head of it around on her lips. He was in total bliss. She looked up at him and smiled. He smiled back.

"Get up and turn around," Prince commanded.

He bent her over the sink and got down on his knees behind her. With both hands he spread her ass cheeks apart and used his index finger to play with her pussy. She moaned as he used his finger to wet the lips of her pussy.

"You like that? That feels good, huh? Bend over some more."

She bent over exposing her hairy mound. He spread her ass cheeks apart even more.

"Damn that's a beautiful sight!" He put the tip of his dick in between her ass cheeks and slowly began to move it up and down. He stopped and bent over toward her pussy and kissed it. While kissing her pussy he slipped his tongue inside her and began to lick the sensitive walls of her pussy. She began to moan while biting her lips. She arched her back and stuck her butt out as he licked her slowly, causing her to breathe uncontrollably. He began to work his tongue in and out of her hole, flicking it back and forth. Her hands gripped the edge of the sink tightly as she rose up, now on her tippy-toes. Prince stopped and stood up behind her, then put the head of his dick between the folds of her pussy and began to rub it against her wetness. He worked the head in slowly and she gripped the sink even tighter. With one hard, powerful thrust, he forced his entire dick into her. She let out a small scream. He slammed himself all the way into her up to the hilt. She tried to move forward, away from him, but the sink held her in place as she let out loud groaning sounds. He then slowly began to work in and out of her, gradually picking up his momentum. She settled down and began to move in rhythm with him.

"Yes, yes, yes," she repeated.

She got louder as his thrusts picked up speed, and he began to slam into her harder and harder. Suddenly he pulled out of her and told her to get down on her knees. She followed his command and opened her mouth and began to suck on his dick again. His legs began to shake. He had to hold on to the wall to keep from buckling to the floor as he shot his hot load into her mouth. Her eyes became watery, but she took it all in and swallowed like a French whore on Hunts Point.

While Prince was in ecstasy, James walked over to the bed and grabbed the little boy's arm and pulled him off the bed. "Now unless you start talking, this little motherfucker is going to start losing some fingers!"

James took his knife out and put the boy's hand on the dresser.

"Motherfucker, you think I'm joking?" James asked with a demented look in his eyes.

He put the knife over the boy's fingers and began to apply pressure. The kid screamed out in pain.

"Okay, okay, downstairs in the living room, move the coffee table, and lift the floorboard up."

THE NEXT MORNING AT CAT'S apartment, they were still up counting the money. It took them another fourteen hours to finish counting the $11 million. The three of them took $3 million apiece and gave Gamble $2 million.

Gamble could hardly contain himself. "For this I'll make sure that you can't lose out with Cynthia!"

Cat laughed and patted him on the back. "I appreciate dat."

"No, I appreciate this!" Gamble replied, holding up a stack of Benjamin's.

ELEVEN

Cat, Prince, and James decided to split up until their next jux. James and Prince felt that it would be safest to take the train. Prince got off in Atlanta and James continued on to New York.

The cab pulled in front of James's house at about midnight. He paid the driver, got his bags out of the trunk, and went inside. There he found Symone asleep on the bed. He got on the bed and began to kiss her, awakening her. She was happy to see him.

After some more kissing, he sat up on the bed. "I got a surprise for you."

He took her hand and led her downstairs to the living room where his bags were on the floor. After sitting her on the couch, he turned the lights on, then dragged one of the bags over to the couch and opened it. Her eyes lit up at the sight of all the money that was in it.

"Baby, you did real good. I knew you could do it."

He smiled as he reached into the bag and opened the side pocket inside it. He pulled out the ring and held it up in front of her.

He handed it to her. "You happy?"

The diamond had much more clarity than the engagement ring that he had bought her.

She took the ring and slid it onto her finger. "Where did you get all this?"

"Let's just say that I had to jux and Prince had to fuck some rich Chinese bitch for it."

She turned and looked at him with her eyes narrowed, trying to get a sense if he was serious. He did not look back at her.

"Well, for shit like this, you can rob and fuck whoever you want, anytime!"

He looked at her and began to laugh. "You crazy!"

"Nah, you crazy!"

THE NEXT DAY JAMES COUNTED some money and put it into a bag. He took the bag with him into his car and headed for LeFrak City. Twenty minutes later he pulled up on the block where he was shot. His men Kaizer and Ant were out there doing their usual thing. All heads were turning as the brand new gold BMW 7 Series turned the corner, shimmering. Everything seemed to move in slow motion as Kaizer put his fist to his mouth.

"That's one mean piece of machine right there!" Kaizer said.

James stepped out of the car.

"Is this nigga for real? Oh, shit! Look at this motherfucker!" Ant said as he and Kaizer began to walk toward James.

"How the fuck you gone do it like that, my nigga?" asked Ant.

James smiled as they hugged and gave each other five.

"Nah, you not that nigga, you that other nigga. How the fuck you gone almost get your head popped off and then months later pull up on the same block like this as if nothing ever happened? You 'bout your shit for real, dawg. You need to let a nigga know how you do what you do 'cause this block shit ain't doing it like that. Motherfucking superman, what's the deal, my nigga?"

"Nothing much, just here."

Kaizer, who was not much of the talking type, was already rolling up a blunt for them.

"I came to see you in the hospital but they got on some shit that only family members was able to visit you because they ain't know who shot you," said Ant.

"So what's really good with you?" asked Kaizer as he passed James the blunt.

"Nothing much, just the same ol' same ol'."

"Well, I'm glad to see that you bounced back from *that* like a champ. That shit was a close one, and the fucked-up thing is a nigga couldn't even help you out, besides calling the ambulance."

"Don't sweat it, fam, that was good enough. I'm here because of that call. So what's good with y'all?"

"Same shit, just out here trying to make some ends meet. Shit been hot for the last four months. These fucking pigs stay trying to lock a nigga up," said Ant.

"What's up, y'all niggaz ain't too busy right now, is you?"

"For you, a nigga never too busy."

"Come on, I want y'all niggaz to take a ride with me."

The three of them got into James's car and lit up another blunt.

"This is some serious shit here, my nigga!" said Kaizer.

"You like this shit?"

"What! Are you for real? This shit here is mean, man!"

"Guess what?"

"What?"

"It's yours."

Kaizer's eyes narrowed as he looked over at James. "Stop playing."

"I ain't playing, my nigga, this shit is yours, and that's real talk, my nigga."

"Come on, gimme the keys, let me whip this bitch," Kaizer said to test James's sincerity.

James opened the door and got out, then reentered the car on the passenger's side. Kaizer climbed over to the driver's seat and started the car.

"That's what's up! Good fuckin' looking, my nigga. What's up? Where we going?"

"Take me to my crib," James said.

As they got on the highway, the blunt was lit and the smoke permeated the interior of the car.

James turned to Ant. "So what's up with your music thing?"

"You know, I want to do that shit but I got bills to pay and that hustling shit just takes up all my damn time."

"Well, listen, you my dog and I want to see you do your thing. I don't want to be talking to you years from now and hear you singing the same damn song. Because you and I both know these streets will do it to you. You both seen how close I came to not being here no more, so here is what I'ma do for you. I'm gonna help you get your shit on."

"Say word!"

"Word."

Ant nodded his head. "That's what's up, my nigga."

"I'ma take care of your bills so you ain't got that as an excuse, so just tell me what you need."

Ant took a deep breath, unable to believe what was happening. "Well, you know that kid Hassan?"

"The one who be making them beats?"

"Yeah!"

"What's up?"

"Well, he is my producer and he need some new equipment for these beats. From there we gonna mix this album down and start to shop it. I already got a plug up at Uni. But it's like if you ain't got no bread, they ain't trying to fuck with you. Niggas be wanting some dough to give you that plug, and that's what I gots to hit this nigga wit."

"Well, don't sweat it, playboy. I got you. What your man Hassan need?"

"He needs some new boards, and that new Triton Studio series keyboard and a drum set."

"Just give me a price and it's done. In the meantime pass me that bag next to you."

Ant picked up the bag next to him and passed it over to James.

"I got one hundred thousand dollars in here. Y'all niggaz split this shit and get off the block before y'all end up with some unwanted drug case," said James.

They pulled up at James's house and he went in and came back out about twenty minutes later with another bag in his hand.

"Take me to that car dealer up on Queens Boulevard."

"Car dealer, what for?"

"You done bagged me for my whip, so I need a new one."

They all laughed.

After several days in LeFrak City, Banit was unsuccessful in his attempts to run into James. He had just missed him on several occasions, according to some of James's friends. But Banit was wasting too much time and not focusing on what he really wanted to do, his priority number one, which was to get back at Cloud. Banit figured that he could pick up Cloud's trail at the precinct they took Banit to at the time of his arrest.

The 112th Precinct was five blocks from Seventy-first Street and Continental Avenue. This was an upscale neighborhood in Queens, one of the more expensive areas to live in, with convenient access to mass transit. It had four movie theaters, an assortment of boutiques and restaurants, as well as a comic-book store, antiques shops, and a wax museum. This was all surrounded by high-rise apartment buildings with overly expensive rent.

A chill went up Banit's spine as he caught a flashback of the day he was brought to the 112th. Banit walked across the street and passed the precinct and the buildings that surrounded it. He did not know exactly what he was looking for, but he wanted to familiarize himself with the area. When he got to the end of the block, he stopped at the corner and looked at his watch. He knew that there were three shifts, 7 a.m. to 3 p.m., 3 p.m. to 11 p.m., and 11 p.m. to 7 a.m. There were also three shifts in between shifts. These officers came on three hours ahead of the regular shift to ensure that an officer was always up to speed with what was going on and to prevent confusion during the shift change that could allow a prisoner to take advantage. These officers did not normally go out onto the streets.

Banit didn't think Cloud would be on this shift because he was active in the field. It did not make sense to be walking back and forth outside all day so he decided to go check out a movie in one of the theaters in the area. This would kill some time until the next shift change. He left the movie at a quarter to two and walked at a moderate pace toward the precinct. Whenever he felt that he was moving too fast, he would do some window-shopping at the many boutiques in the area. He timed himself so that he would be by the precinct fifteen minutes to three. Fortunately, he didn't have to be in front of the precinct because it was located on a one-way street, which meant that all traffic would have to come from his direction. He figured in three shifts he would be able to make Cloud out.

After an hour, the shift change was completed, but Banit had had no luck in spotting Cloud. It would be another seven hours before the next shift change. He needed to find something to do until then. Since LeFrak City was only fifteen minutes away by car, he opted to go back there to try his luck with James again.

CAT PULLED UP AT THE Metro apartment complex where Cynthia lived to pick her up for their date. He waited in the lobby for her to come downstairs. Looking out at the pool, he did not notice her when she got off the elevator.

"I think I can recognize you from any angle," she said, standing only two feet from him.

He spun around to see her standing there looking gorgeous in a black dress. Her hair was done straight, flowing over her shoulders and down her back. She hardly had any makeup on, allowing her natural beauty to stand out.

"You look absolutely stunning," said Cat.

"And you look well yourself." Her radiant smile warmed his heart.

Frozen in time, with difficulty he unlocked his joints as she moved toward him for a hug. They embraced each other, and her perfume reached his nostrils, sending his mind racing with all sorts of lustful thoughts.

"Shall we be going?" said Cat.

"I'm ready."

Cat had got his hands on a pair of tickets to see Brian McKnight at the Sandals hotel. It was dubbed "Ladies Night at the Sandals." They were seated up front in the first row left of the stage. The two opening acts were a local talent and the other from North Carolina. When Brian came on to perform, ushers went around the room giving every lady a rose. Brian's last song was dedicated to Cynthia, which Cat had paid for in advance. McKnight walked off the stage and to their table as he sang 'Back at One.' Cat scored big with this move.

After the show they ordered their food. Cynthia selected a seafood platter of clams, lobster tails, and pink salmon. Cat also decided on seafood.

"You know what they say about seafood?" asked Cat.

"What's that?"

"It has a way of peaking certain hormones."

"Is that right?"

"That's right, so my advice is not to indulge too much."

"Well, my cousin did say to be extra nice to you, which is a first. You must've left one hell of an impression on him because he has always been overprotective of me. This might lead to a *very* interesting night."

"Is that so?"

"I think so." She smiled.

"So you're saying that you don't find the night interesting thus far?"

"No, that's not what I'm saying. I think you missed the key word."

"Which is?"

"Which is *very*. The night has certainly been interesting, and the way things are going, it could get *very*." She ended her sentence with another smile and an inviting stare into his eyes.

After dinner, they drove down the beach for a stroll on the boardwalk. Shortly thereafter, Cynthia wanted to walk on the beach. They took off their shoes and hit the sand. They played the game of letting the waves chase their feet, which reminded Cat of his childhood in Jamaica. As they ran from the oncoming water, Cat grabbed hold of Cynthia, spun her around, and took her back into the water to get her feet wet. She tried holding her feet up so they wouldn't touch the water, but he kept lowering her. Overwhelmed, Cynthia quickly threw her arms around Cat's neck and held on tight. In one last attempt to keep from getting wet, she wrapped her legs around his waist. Now the only way to get her into the water was for him to lie down in the water with her. Cat was enjoying this position. He could sense she did as well, through all the laughing and yelling at him.

"No, you won't get me!"

"Oh, I won't?"

"Nope."

He walked farther out into the water, his arms wrapped around her, helping her stay straddled to him. Suddenly their laughter slowed and she began to stare into his eyes.

"So, what should I formally know you as?"

He smiled. "Neil Johnson. And as long as you keep it a secret, you'll be the only one permitted to use it."

"I guess I should feel privileged."

"Let's just say I'm a very private person."

"So what did you do that you need to be running around with a new identity?"

"Things just got a little heated back home."

"And I guess back home would be New York?"

"Yes, but give it some time and everything will be fine."

She looked deep into his eyes as if she were looking into his soul. "I know a lot of women who fell for a line like that. They got themselves all wrapped up in a man who was not living on the right side of the law, only to be left alone one day with a bunch of baggage—babies, bills, and a whole lot of unhealthy emotions. Would that be what I'm in for?"

"I promise I would not leave you like that," Cat proclaimed with all the sincerity he could muster.

She narrowed her eyes, looking skeptical and apprehensive.

"Tell you what. How about we go back to my apartment and spend the rest of the night together?" Cat suggested.

"That sounds good, even though I have this strange feeling that I'm about to fall off of a cliff."

They smiled at each other knowingly, as if they shared some inside joke.

They left the beach and went to Cat's apartment. He opened the door and said teasingly, "After you, lady."

"Thank you, gentleman," she replied with a smirk.

He escorted her to the living room and asked her to have a seat on the couch. He sat next to her and turned on the radio. Marvin Gaye's "Let's Get It On" began to play softly in the background.

"You know that I haven't been with a man in almost two years?"

"And why is that?"

"I don't know. I guess I just grew tired of their bullshit."

"And now?"

She paused for a moment to contemplate her response. "There seems to be something about you. I don't know what makes you different, but I find you intriguing."

"I didn't know that I had that effect."

"Well, you do."

As they stared at each other, Cat casually reached over and touched her face. She looked deep into his eyes and smiled, placing her hands over his. Slowly he pulled her toward him and placed his lips on hers. Her lips were full and soft and moist. Her body quivered as she kissed him back. He kissed her again, not pulling away, holding her close to him. She held him tightly, kissing him passionately, her heart pounding against his chest.

Slowly he slid his hands up her inner thighs and under the hem of her dress until he touched her panties. She seemed a bit overwhelmed as she jerked a little, but then relaxed just as quickly. He reached over and helped her out of her dress. His dick began to harden. She felt her nipples harden as her pussy became moist, then wet. She took off her bra as he bent over and pulled her panties down to the floor. She stepped out of them, pushing him back away from her. Cat stood back, admiring her well-sculptured frame. He began to undress quickly, throwing his clothing to the floor. In no time, the both of them were nude.

In unison, they moved toward the bed. From behind her, Cat pulled Cynthia closer to him and began to kiss her neck and shoulders. He reached his hands around her and began to squeeze and massage her breasts.

"Turn around, I wanna taste you," he said.

She did. He began to kiss her lips, slowly moving down to her breasts, then down to her stomach, gently biting her as he went along. She moaned in response to the touch of his lips, arching her back as she lay down ready for him. She was dripping wet. Cat licked softly at first, then harder, and the more he licked her wet pussy, the harder she moaned.

"Yes, Cat," she moaned, squirming. Her

juices flowed, filling his mouth. He continued to lick, working his way back up her stomach, then to her breasts and her neck, until their lips were joined again.

"Oooooh," she whispered into his ears as she felt his dick slide inside her. She wanted him so badly she almost screamed. Once his dick was deep inside her, he began to fuck her, fast and hard. She loved the feeling of his dick ramming in and out of her. In and out, in and out, again and again. She begged him to not ever stop. He made love to her harder and deeper until she came with a cry of ecstatic pleasure. She pushed him off, rolling him onto his back. She began to suck his dick, working it in and out of her mouth, licking the shaft with her tongue.

"Oh, shit, oh, shit, I'm cumming, baby."

She pulled his dick out of her mouth and begin to jerk it until he released his load all over her breasts and stomach.

"Damn, that was good," he said.

"Oh, I loved it, too," she whispered into his ears.

BANIT WENT BACK TO THE precinct at eleven, but still had no luck. He returned at seven the next morning, but still nothing. For a full week Banit went back and forth between LeFrak City and the precinct looking for James and Cloud. He decided to try the other end of the block to see if he might catch Cloud leaving work, but still he had no luck. He tried the three in-between shifts and again came up with nothing. He decided to give it one last try.

To kill a few hours before the shift change, Banit stopped off at a twenty-four-hour diner two blocks from the precinct. He sat at the back of the diner and ordered two eggs with cheese on a plain bagel with a cup of coffee. Here was the man who pulled off one of the most daring escapes in the city's history, sitting in a diner about to piss his freedom away. He should have been long gone over one of the borders by now.

Banit thought about killing Cloud, but surely that would only bring more heat. He wouldn't be able to hide anywhere on earth—well, maybe Cuba. Yes, life in America was over for him, but with the money he had left, he could certainly live comfortably in some small, insignificant village somewhere. Maybe that was what he should have been concentrating on instead of his foolish revenge plan.

Perhaps he should just find James and warn his uncle and Cat about Cloud, then get the fuck out of town. If he could make it back to Jamaica with his money, he would be good. He could buy a piece of land and build a decent house and start up a chicken farm or open up a grocery store or something. Then maybe find himself a chick who don't want to do nothing but fuck. He smiled at the thought, but he still wanted to look that bastard Cloud in his eyes one more time. "Fuck it, I'll just try to find James," he said to himself as he took the last bite of his sandwich.

"Hey, Vinny . . . give me the usual."

Banit, recognizing the voice, looked up from his plate. The hair on his arms began to rise. He looked up over the divider at the man sitting at the counter. His back was to Banit. The man had on a black leather cap similar to the one Cloud always wore. He turned his face a bit to the side, and Banit got a look at his face and was sure that the voice belonged to none other than Cloud. Banit's mission was reinvigorated.

He watched Cloud closely as he ate. When he was finished, Cloud paid for his food and walked out. Banit quickly got up and went to the counter.

"What's the price . . . ?"

"That will be eight fifty-nine."

Banit pulled out a ten-dollar bill. "Keep the change," he said as he rushed out.

Banit got outside just in time to see Cloud getting into a blue Mustang. He watched the car as it drove in the direction of the precinct. Banit quickly ran around the corner and got into his stolen Dodge Stratus. He lost sight of Cloud, but drove by the precinct hoping to pick up his trail. Not seeing the blue Mustang, Banit made a right and circled the block. He went down another street, where he finally spotted the blue Mustang parked about ten cars from the corner.

TWELVE

James told Symone to go ahead and make wedding plans. He had taken the ring that he had got from the last jux to get it appraised. While doing so, he got it cleaned and engraved with JAMES LOVES SYMONE. The ring was valued at $30,000.

Soon thereafter, James flew back to Miami for another jux. On the first-class flight, James was thinking about how far he had come from his days of hustling weed on the block with Kaizer and Ant. He had made some money, but it was hard to hold on to. He spent it just as fast as he made it, as if it just slipped through his hands. If their drug spot wasn't getting busted, the competition was heating up the spot by shooting at it. There was always drama and beef. James was fed up with making his money that way, especially when one of his workers got killed in retaliation.

It was then he found his calling as a stickup kid. He and his right-hand man, Kell from Brooklyn, went to Philadelphia and opened up shop. Their first victim was a local drug dealer called Ching—because of his Asian-like features—who was getting his weight from New York at a much higher price than they were. He was unable to compete with James and them, so he decided to shoot up their spot and make things hot for them. James chose to retaliate. Kell, on the other hand, felt that retaliating wouldn't be the best thing to do at that moment. After hearing that, James went at it alone.

From one of the crackheads in town, he found out where Ching lived. The following night he drove to Ching's house. The block seemed almost deserted. James knocked twice on the door, and a few moments later he heard the locks clicking. He quickly reached into his waistband for his gun before the door was opened all the way. The woman in front of him stood about five feet six inches and could have passed for Halle Berry's sister.

"Yes?"

James wasn't sure what to say. Perhaps he was at the wrong house. He took a quick look over his shoulder to see if anyone was behind him or on the streets.

"Ah, is Ching here?"

"Yeah, he's here. What you want, some weight?" He couldn't believe that she would ask him a question like that when she had no idea who or what he was.

"Yeah, I need some weight."

"All right, come in and close the door behind you."

I could blow her brains out right now. But James wanted to see where the whole thing would lead. He walked in and closed the door behind him. Looking around the living room, he saw no sign of anyone besides her.

"So, where's Ching?"

"I think that fat motherfucker's in the bathroom taking a shit."

After hearing that, he tucked the gun in the small of his back.

"I ain't never seen you before," she said.

"I'm a new customer. Ching told me to meet him here."

"Which part of town you work?"

"I'm over on the corner of 52nd and Chestnut."

"Damn! Ain't it crazy hot over there?"

Yeah, your fucking man is the reason why it's hot. James felt the urge to pull out his gun and shoot her right there, then go and kill Ching while he was on the toilet. "Yes, but there's a lot of money over there. I just be moving in and out."

"Well, that fat nigga might be shitting all night. If you want me to take care of you, that's cool."

"That sounds good."

"All right then, come with me."

In the back, a table and three chairs were in the middle of the room. James located the bathroom to the left of the living room as he walked down the hall to the back room.

"So how much you want?" she asked James.

"I'ma need a quarter."

"You talking a quarter bird?"

"Yeah, every two days."

"Damn, things must be really moving over there." She walked over to the closet and opened it. "Have a seat, I'll be right with you."

She reached in the closet for a bag and turned around.

"Shhh," said James with one finger at his lips and his gun in her face.

She looked as if she wanted to cry. He told her not to make a sound, then asked her where the rest of the drugs were. She told him that they were all in the closet. James asked her where the money was, and she told him that it was also inside the closet. He looked around the room and could not find anything to put the drugs and money into. He looked at her and told her to take her clothes off.

"Hurry up!" he barked.

She quickly took off her sweatpants and top. He told her to tie the bottom of the legs of her pants and to start dropping the cocaine and money inside the legs of her sweatpants. Once they were full, he pulled the string at the waist and tied it tightly. He then used her top to tie her hands behind her back. When he was done, he noticed that water was coming down her legs.

"Just do everything I tell you and everything will be fine. Let's go."

As he walked her into the hall, he heard the toilet flush. When he got to the living room, he told her to sit on the couch and be quiet. James put the sweatpants down by the other couch and went and stood by the bathroom and waited for the door to open. As soon as it opened, he put the gun in Ching's face and pulled him into the living room on the floor. He lay on his back with his hands up attempting to protect his head.

"You shot up the wrong nigga's spot, fat boy!" said James as he pistol-whipped Ching with the butt of the gun. The blood spurt out of Ching's face and head. The carpet was crimson red when James was done beating him. The girl was crying, begging him to stop. James beat

Ching until he was unrecognizable. No one fucked with James's money. That was the message he wanted to send. He had to make an example of Ching. He needed to send a shocking message, and she'd spread the word on what he did to Ching.

JAMES'S PLANE LANDED IN MIAMI that afternoon. He took a taxi to Cat's apartment. When he got there, Prince had already arrived. They got down to business right away, planning their next jux. Cat had been scoping it out while they were out of town. The target was a Jewish man who owned a chain of video stores. He specialized in pornography. His specialty was black-market tapes, the kind that were illegal in the United States. Whatever your fetish was, he was able to get his hands on it. Two mayors had already tried to shut him down, but neither of them were successful. They only increased his business by generating publicity, causing more people to become interested. The Jewish man liked to party and gamble, too.

The target lived in an exclusive Jewish community with its own security force. He didn't live in a huge, fancy house, as were many of the houses in the area. His was a simple two-story house with a basement.

An Audi S4 was stolen for the job. Cat

liked Audis for their ability to withstand merciless driving. They parked two blocks over and trekked to the house through backyards and over fences. Once in the backyard they checked out the basement windows, which had cemented bars on them. The first-floor windows had shutters. They had never before come across such a fortified house. Something valuable was definitely inside. They grouped up in the bushes at the back of the house.

"This might have to be a rush job," said Cat.

"It looks that way," replied Prince.

Cat looked up at the second-floor windows and noticed they didn't have any shutters on them.

"We should try to get to one of those windows." Cat pointed. "We could make a human ladder with the three of us. We should be able to reach that bitch."

Prince looked up trying to get a measurement. "That shit just might fucking work."

"Come on, let's give it a try," said Cat.

The three of them crept along quietly until they were directly under one of the second-floor windows that faced the back of the house.

"Since we making this human ladder, that means only one of us is going to be able to get inside the house. So whoever goes in first is gonna have to get control of the house all by himself," said Prince.

"I got it," said James.

"All right then, that's settled," replied Cat. "You gotta be quick. Once everything is settled, throw us down a sheet to come up."

Cat leaned against the wall first, then Prince climbed onto his shoulders. James then climbed onto Cat's back, then up onto Prince's shoulders. He was right at the window. The lights inside the house were off and he was unable to see through the windows. The weight of the both of them on his shoulders began to break Cat out into a sweat. He wanted to step forward a bit to take some of the pressure from his lower back, but he was at a perfect thirty-degree angle and knew that if he moved, he could send both of them tumbling to the ground. He bit his lip and held on to the wall. James gave a push at the window and it came open. As he pushed it farther, suddenly a loud bang rang out. It didn't take long to register in James's mind and with the rest of the crew that the banging sounds were gunshots. There was another bang and the window shattered. James lost his grip and went crashing to the ground below. Prince lost his balance and went tumbling to the ground after him. Somebody from inside the house was shooting at them. Prince got to his feet quickly, and he and Cat drew their guns and aimed at the window. Prince fired a warning shot to prevent the person from coming to the window and opening fire on them while they were uncovered. James had taken a hard fall. He was still on the ground, struggling to get to his feet. Prince quickly went to his aid, helping him up.

"Who shot?"

"I don't know."

"Come on, get up!"

Cat kept his gun aimed at the window. James got to his feet and Prince helped him toward the fence at the back of the house. Cat followed, walking backward with his gun still trained on the window. Suddenly, more shots were fired from the window. Cat returned fire, then Prince did the same. James drew his gun and aimed and fired as well. They lit the window up like a stadium. The sound of sirens in the distance became more clear as the seconds went by.

"What the fuck!"

"Come on, let's move it."

They got over the fence and picked up the pace through the backyards leading to their car. Cat was the driver. James jumped in the back and Prince in the front passenger seat. They removed their masks as the car got on its way. Cat drove the speed limit to avoid unwanted attention. When they got to the next corner, they were met by a patrol car from the neighborhood security. They drove straight. As they passed the car, the driver stared at them. The car made a right and began to follow them. Suddenly the lights came on, signaling them to pull over.

"Shit! That's that nigga on us!" yelled Cat.

He stepped on the clutch and found the fourth gear. He then came up off the clutch and punched the gas to the floor. The Audi rapidly accelerated as if it were ready to be mistreated. The patrol car gave chase. It gained on them as they twisted and turned through the corners and streets.

"We have to slow dem down before we touch the highway," Cat announced.

Prince reached into his pouch for another clip. He pressed the release button on his Browning nine-millimeter and dropped the clip out. He inserted the new clip and released the select button. He then put the window down.

"Hold my legs," he said to James.

James reached over the front seat and took hold of Prince's legs as he climbed out of the window and sat on the door with half his body outside. He took aim at the security car and began to fire into its engine. The car began to swerve and shortly veered off the road into the woods, hitting a tree.

Prince began to laugh. "Yeah, motherfuckers!"

They got onto the highway and slowed to a

normal speed. They stopped off to pick up Cat's car, then ditched the Audi, wiping it clean before heading back to Cat's place.

"Whoever it was, they must've heard us trying to climb up the side of the house," said James.

"You know, you one lucky motherfucker, kid," said Cat to James. "That fucker could have taken your head off."

"That nigga must really have something big he hiding up in there with all that goddamn security," said Prince.

"Listen, we got to take that place tomorrow," said Cat.

"I know you ain't talking about going back there," replied James, seeing this mishap as a second warning that he should leave his life of crime behind.

"That's exactly what I'm talking about. We gotta rush the place. He definitely has something in there, and we have to get it. I don't think we'll ever be able to crawl in on him, especially after tonight. We have to take him while we still can. By tomorrow morning, the police will be finished with gathering their information and evidence. He and the security people won't even be thinking that we would be so brazen as to come back the very next day. They will have their guard down. All we need to do is catch him with his keys in the door and we got him."

There was a silence for a while after Cat finished.

"Fuck it, let's do this!" Prince said.

They both looked at James. He shrugged his shoulders.

"Okay, then let's set up for it. James, you get some rest while me and Prince go get us another car."

They were back in two hours with a Volvo S80. It was equipped with eight cylinders, all-wheel drive, Volvo's Four-C active-drive suspension, and the twin turbo-boost 340 horses. They parked it at the back of Cat's building. Back in the house, the three men discussed the rush job. They decided that they would take the Jew after he closed the store and was heading home.

The following day they were set and ready two hours before the store was to close. The Jew's car was parked on the side of the store. They parked across the street and waited, watching for the store to close. They spotted him at closing time. The last worker left after helping him pull down the gates. He put the locks on and walked around the corner toward his vehicle. They tailed him from a distance. Halfway into the ride home, he made an abrupt turn.

"What the fuck is he doing?" asked James.

"I don't know. Maybe he's making another stop before he heads home," said Prince.

"Maybe he's going to get a bigger gun," James said.

They all laughed at that. They followed him to another neighborhood, where he made a few turns before pulling up in front of a house. They parked about a half block away and watched as he got out of his car with a bag in his hand and hurried up to the front door, where he flipped through his keys and used them to enter the house.

"What's this?" asked Cat. "This might be the stash house here. What do you think?"

"It could be. Anything is possible fucking with this dude here," replied Prince.

"So what now?" asked James, concerned for their safety.

"I think we should take him here," said Prince.

"I think so, too. Let's move," Cat said.

The sun was still up and the day was bright. They definitely looked strange dressed in all black with baseball caps and gloves. They took a quick survey of the windows on the houses close by. No one seemed to be looking out. They quickly walked into the yard and took cover at the side of the house, behind the bushes, not too far from the door. Fifteen minutes later they heard the door opening. Cat peeped around the corner of the house to see a man with his back turned locking the door. Cat gave the signal and they all pulled their masks over their faces and pulled their guns from their waistbands. They wasted no time running from the side of the house to the door, where they jumped on top of the guy. They pushed him inside and closed the door behind them. Cat and Prince were subduing him while James quickly ran through the house to see if anyone else was inside. After binding the man's hands and feet, Prince went to the windows and looked out at the surrounding houses to see if anyone had seen them.

James came back to the living room. "Everything is clear."

"Everything looks clear here as well," said Prince.

After sitting the man in a chair, James looked at him and said, "We got you, motherfucker!" He punched the man in his face. "That's for almost killing me, you motherfucker!"

"You work on him while we give the house a sweep," said Cat.

"This is going to be fun," James chided, pounding his fist into his other hand. James got ready to punch the man in the face again, but he flinched.

"Don't! Please don't! Tell me what you want and it's yours," he pleaded.

"You're not talking fast enough!"

"In the kitchen . . . in the deep freezer . . . remove the meats and there you'll find the money."

"You heard that?" yelled James to Prince.

"Loud and clear, Houston," said Prince.

He and Cat went into the kitchen and did as the man said. Under the meat were six rows of cash that went to the bottom of the freezer. In the trash can was the plastic bag the old man had earlier brought with him into the house.

"So that's what he had in the bag," Cat said, referring to the money in the freezer. They began to remove the money from the freezer, putting it into garbage bags.

"How much money is here?" asked James.

"Eight million," the man replied in a trembling voice.

"Damn, that's a lot of bread there."

After they finished putting the money in the bags, Cat called James into the kitchen where he and Prince were.

"This was too easy. I still want to hit his house. I think he's hiding something there. Something big."

"So what's the plan?" asked Prince.

"James, you stay here while me and Prince go to the house. We have his keys so we can walk right in on whoever is there."

They went back out to the living room where the man was.

"Okay, Mr. Gunman, here is the deal," Cat said. "We are going to your house, where I'm sure the rest of it is. Now you can tell us where in the house it is and make it easy on your wife or whoever's in there. Or, you can make it a long day for her or whoever, your choice. Get my drift?"

The target took a deep breath. "Slide the mattress off the bed in the master bedroom. The board on the box spring slides off, the rest of it is there."

"How much?"

"Nine million."

"We are not taking any chances. We gonna take his car and take this money to my place, and then head on over to his house for the rest. Once we have everything, we gonna call you here. Just hop in the Volvo and meet us back at my place. You dig?"

Cat then turned to the man and asked him for the number to the house. From there they were off.

Three hours later, James began to grow impatient. "Where are they? Hurry up and call, damn it!" he said, pacing back and forth in the living room wondering if he should just leave. Walk away from everything.

The sun had gone down. He walked over and checked the man's restraints. Another half hour passed and no call.

"I swear if they don't call in the next fifteen minutes, I'm outta here," James said under his breath.

He walked over to the window and looked outside to make sure all was still clear.

AT THE HOUSE, PRINCE AND Cat had got in without any problems. They found the Jew's wife in the kitchen. She didn't hear them when they came in. She did not scream or seem to be startled when she turned around and saw them there with their guns out. She was calm, as if she was expecting them. She placed the knife she was using on the counter. Without a word, she walked past them, heading upstairs toward the master bedroom.

"You are the men that were here last night?" she asked.

"Yes."

"How is my husband?"

"He is fine. You have nothing to worry about. All we came for is the money," said Cat.

"If only such brave hearts could be put to work for God," she said.

Prince walked over to the bed and flipped the mattress off. He slid the board cover off.

The money was there. They bagged the money and got ready to leave. When they got to the door and looked out the window, they noticed a security car sitting out front.

"What the fuck are they doing there?" asked Prince.

"You think we've been spotted?"

"Nah, I don't think so, this whole place would have been surrounded already."

They waited for an hour trying to wait the police out. They showed no signs of leaving.

"We can't just sit here all night long, and we can't have our man sitting there all this time without hearing from us. He is going to think something went wrong," said Cat.

"Go ahead and make the call," said Cat.

Prince picked the phone up and called James. He answered on the first ring.

"Breeze!" said Prince.

James hung up the phone and put his gun in his waistband, then walked over to the Jew and slapped him in his face with all his might. "Pussy, that's for almost killing me again," James said before exiting the house.

Cat was becoming impatient. "Look, you know da deal, we have to blaze our way out of here."

"Let's do this," replied Prince.

They picked up the bags, and with their guns in their hands they unlocked the door.

"You ready?"

"Come on, let's do it!"

Just as they opened the door, ready to start shooting, the car began to drive off. They looked at each other and smiled.

"That was a close call. Let's get the fuck out of here," said Prince.

After meeting up with James at Cat's apartment, they went and ditched the cars. The money was split, $4.25 million for each of them.

The next day Cat delivered Gamble's share to him.

"What happened? You had me worried. You was supposed to call me yesterday and you didn't. I was stuck on the news channel all day and night."

"Man, if you only knew the half. You are very lucky to be getting this right now."

Cat gave Gamble the whole rundown on everything that went down.

"You motherfuckers are a serious piece of work! I have nothing but the utmost respect for y'all. I'm telling you, keep having success like this and it won't be long before we can retire from this business. I could go and buy me a yacht and sail the world like I dream of doing."

Cat laughed.

"So how did it go with my cousin?"

"Everything went just fine. Thanks for putting in that word for me."

"Don't mention it, I told you that I would."

"Yeah, but good looking out, though. Listen, I need to find me another apartment. There's been way too much movement by me and my people where I'm at right now. I need to get a house, something out of sight."

"That's no problem at all, I know the perfect place! When will you need it?"

"ASAP."

"Say no more, we'll go and look at it tomorrow. Right now I gots to go out and put all this cheddar away."

The crew pulled off another five juxes before splitting up for a break. Three of the juxes provided them with more cash, but two did not. The three successful ones netted a total of $6 million apiece. Everybody went his separate way for a while.

THIRTEEN

Cloud remained on the hunt for Cat and his crew. It had become personal for him. Recapturing Banit and catching the rest of the fraternity became his life's goal. Banit's escape brought the serial-robbery case a lot of attention. The police staked out The Lodge, but still were unable to come up with any leads.

The correction officers that helped in the escape had their lives turned inside out and put under a microscope. Michael's partner decided to retire with his $250,000 and his pension. Michael decided that he would stick it out. He wanted to show that he had nothing to do with it. Some of the inmates on the bus that morning of the escape identified Banit as being on the bus. One of them told the investigators that he simply walked off, away from the bus once they got to court. But Michael stuck to his guns saying that Banit never got on the bus that morning, that the screwup had to have happened at Rikers Island. The investigators found it highly unlikely that he escaped from the Island. It would have been too many checkpoints to go through without some inside help. They concluded that it had to have taken place the way the inmates said, that he walked off the bus. And if he had done that, he had to have had help.

The word of an inmate was not going to hold up in court without some hard evidence to back it up. The police decided not to press charges until they could do exactly that. Michael had been careful enough to slip Banit's paperwork from the pile of court papers and left them back on Rikers Island, so as far as he was concerned, Banit was never on his bus.

Despite many setbacks, Cloud did not stop pursuing the case. He didn't spend enough time with Prince to learn his real name or get an address on him. All he had was a description. He knew James was not with them for long, so if he was captured, he would not be charged with as many robberies as the rest. This made James less important than the other crew members. On the other hand, James could possibly lead the police to the rest of them.

The crew could be anywhere by now. Under

the pressure of his superiors, Cloud made calls to many different police departments in different states to see if any robberies fit the pattern of the crew. The closest resemblance was in Philadelphia, but when he went out there to check it out, the evidence did not have the markings of the crew, markings he knew well from his time with them.

It was 7 p.m. and Cloud put in a second shift trying to turn over some stones. He was exhausted and decided to call it quits for the day. He packed up his things, punched out on the clock, and walked out of the precinct to his car. As he pulled out in his car, a Dodge Stratus parked four cars down pulled out shortly behind him.

Cloud got onto the highway and headed toward Long Island. He exited the highway at Roosevelt Field. The Dodge got off, too. No other cars got off with them. Banit and Cloud came up on a red light at the next intersection. Banit didn't want to have to pull up and stop right behind him at the light. Fortunately, the light turned green as Cloud came up on the light.

Banit drove for about seven more blocks behind Cloud on the wide, two-way street. Banit was able to stay about two blocks behind Cloud. Cloud slowed down and made a right. Banit raced to the corner and made the right turn just in time to see Cloud pulling into a driveway. It was the fifth house on the block.

"Got you, motherfucker!" said Banit as he drove on by, feeling ecstatic.

Cloud was at his mercy now. He knew that people tended to relax more in the confines of their home. He would be able to catch Cloud off guard. Now he could put Plan B into motion. First, he needed to find James. He wanted to warn him of Cloud before he got a trail on them.

PRINCE HAD RETURNED TO ATLANTA. With his newfound millions he had made up his mind that he was going to leave the States for Jamaica. From Jamaica, he would go wherever he wanted in the world. Nothing was holding him back. He figured he would leave his mother and his sister some money and be gone for good.

James, on the other hand, never thought of himself as being a wanted man. He went on living his life as though nothing were wrong. While in Miami, he did some thinking after seeing a documentary on J-Prince, a Miami native. James liked how J-Prince came up in the streets and how he crossed over and began to make a killing in the music business. He decided that instead of having Kaizer and Ant sign with just any music company, who would surely be looking to jerk them, they would simply start up their own. He had enough money. They could shoot their own videos, put on their own shows, and do their own promotion. James reasoned that by helping his friends it could be a way out for himself.

After returning to New York, James encouraged Symone to enroll in college after their wedding. He wanted her to major in business. He needed someone he could trust to manage his money.

James had a date with a car dealer. As the cover was slowly pulled from the vehicle, the silence that gripped the showroom floor transformed into oohs and aahs. The wealthy rarely buy cars off the rack. Their car is a way of displaying their wealth. It has to be built or tailored to their specifications. By the looks of this Lamborghini Murciélago, its owner could be saying only one thing: "I have the ability to purchase the most exclusive and valuable vehicle in the world."

James decided to check up on Ant to see what kind of progress he was making. As the galaxy-black Lamborghini rounded the corner of Junction Boulevard and Fifty-seventh Avenue, the sun coming through the high-rises of the LeFrak City complex glistened off its body. It took only one person to notice it, and like a chain reaction word rippled down the long block. All eyes were focused in the same direction at the same time. Like something straight out of a Cash Money video, James cruised down the avenue with the top down paying no one in particular any mind. He was in his best "fronting mode." Not like some rapper who has made his riches legally from the music business and come back to town to front on those that he once ran the streets with, but like a nigga who had earned the right to floss in the hood by coming up on his grind. The car was a sight to behold.

"HEY, PAULO, YOU HAVE A call on four," said the police clerk to Cloud.

"Okay, thank you." Cloud put his pen down and picked up the phone. He pressed the button for line four.

"Yes, this is Detective Williams, out of Miami."

"Yes, Mr. Williams, how may I help you?"

"Well, one of the deputies was going through the national data bank trying to find similarities to a string of robberies that have been taking place here in the past nine months."

A rush of anxiety gripped Cloud's nerves when he heard the detective's words.

"He wasn't sure if your case meant anything or had anything to do with what's been going on here in our city, but we happened to notice similar patterns in a string of robberies that took place up in your neck of the woods."

Cloud was at full attention as he slid his desk drawer open and pulled out the file on The Order case, which he always kept at hand.

"Might any of this ring a bell, partner?"

"Oh, absolutely, please go on, Detective," said Cloud.

"After some more digging he found out that there was a prison escape connected to the case as well as a couple of wanted men."

Cloud's palm literally became slippery on the phone receiver. "Ah, Detective, could you please hold on for one moment?"

"Sure."

Cloud put the detective on hold and called for his superior to pick up the line for a conference call. After briefing the captain on the situation, they both got on the line. The captain introduced himself and the detective continued.

"We believe the wanted men might have relocated to our area and are now operating here."

The three spent another hour on the phone, with the detectives trading notes and case files. The file said there were three men. Cloud knew two of them would be Cat and Prince. Could the third be James? Could it be Banit? As they went on, Cloud became more and more convinced that he had found them. He assured the detective that they would look over the case and would be in touch with him.

After the call, Cloud left his desk and went upstairs to the captain's office, walked in, and sat down.

"So what do you think or make of all this?" asked Cloud.

"I think you might have something here. I know that you have been hard on this investigation and no one knows it better than you. You know the inner workings of their organization and the minds of these guys. No one deserves to close the case more than you."

"Thank you, sir."

"Here is what you're gonna do. You are going to take what you need and fly down to Miami and take a look at what they have to see if it's in fact our guys."

A big smile came across Cloud's face. "Oh, yes, thank you, sir!"

"Don't mention it. Just break the damn case."

"I will break it, sir."

"How soon will you be ready?"

"I'm ready now, sir."

"Well, then you can fly out tomorrow. I'll call the sheriff and let him know of our plans and ask him to make some preparations for you."

Cloud left the office feeling renewed. He

went back to his desk and got together every removable piece of evidence and put them into a box. He then went home and took a shower and packed. When he was done, he lay back on his bed happily thinking about the possibility of seeing Cat and Prince, and hopefully Banit and James. He could hardly wait to get to Miami.

CLOUD'S FLIGHT LANDED AT 1 p.m. The sheriff and the detective met him at the airport and took him to his hotel. After checking into his room and putting his things away, Cloud headed to the station house. He spent the next three hours looking over files filled with notes, evidence, and witness statements. All of the robberies bore the markings of the fraternity. Instinctually, he just knew it was them. He wrapped it up on the ninth hour and went back to his hotel room for the night.

The sheriff assigned Alan Hemming, a deputy familiar with the case, to work with Cloud. Hemming was ready and waiting at 6 a.m. at the hotel on his way to work to pick Cloud up. Tired from his night of research, Cloud was drowsy, but he certainly did not want the sheriff to be waiting on him for long. It would surely reflect poorly on the whole New York Police Department. After checking into the station, Cloud decided to go out and interview some of the witnesses and examine a few crime scenes. Cloud was sure this was the work of The Order. Careful examination of all the evidence compelled the police to form a task force. They decided that around-the-clock attention was needed since most of their work would be done under the cover of night. Cloud had to figure out how The Order was selecting its targets.

The victims all had something or someone in common. All the victims had large amounts of untaxed dollars. Could all these men themselves be part of some organization where a member would know this?

Besides Cloud, the young deputy Hemming knew more about the case than anyone else on the task force. The two put their minds together to figure out the connection among the victims.

THINGS WERE GOING WELL WITH Cat and Cynthia. The two had got close and started to develop stronger feelings for each other. He had moved into his new house, which Gamble had worked out for him. Cynthia helped decorate the place, even though Cat didn't plan on staying there too long. She would spend many evenings there making Cat dinner, hanging out, and discussing their future together.

"Look, like I told you, I'm on the run from the law in New York. Now, let's say I turn myself in and serve time in prison. If you were willing to stand by me until I got out, it would be a really long time. I can't offer you a normal life."

Cynthia looked deep into Cat's eyes as he spoke. It was evident that this would not work out between them. Tears began to build in her eyes.

Cat stepped forward and took Cynthia into his arms. His mind reached for something to say to change the mood in the room.

"But there is a chance," he whispered in her ear.

"What?" she asked, confused.

He pulled back just a bit so he could see her face and look into her eyes.

"There is an alternative," he repeated with a smile.

"What alternative? What are you talking about, an alternative?"

"A normal life is not possible for us in the States, and that's okay because the world is a very big place. Now if you are willing, we could relocate to anywhere. Maybe England, Africa, Paris, South America, anywhere you would like. That is, if you are able to pull away from every attachment you have holding you here. I have more than enough money, more money than you and I could live to spend. You would never have to worry about working a day in your life. We could just live it up from here on out. Of course, you would have to give me a couple of months to put every ting together."

"It all sounds good right now, but I will need some time to think about it." She began to wipe the tears from her eyes.

"There's no rush, take your time, I want you to make the right decision."

Cloud had flown back to New York to file his report with his superiors. While he was away, Deputy Hemming made a discovery that broke the case wide-open for them. He learned from the testimony of one of the victims that at one point or another the victims had all partied together. If not together, then at the same places but at different times. This was definitely the connection they had with one another; the common thread was somewhere in there.

Cloud spent only two days in New York before returning to Miami. As soon as he entered the car, Hemming revealed his discovery of the common link. After checking into the hotel, they headed to the station house to get to work on their new theory.

They called a meeting with the rest of the task force and laid out their revelation. Plans were made to interview the witnesses one more time. This time special attention would be paid to their extracurricular activities. When asked who kept the best parties, almost all of them said Gamble. After digging into who this Gamble character was, they identified him as "the man" when it came to partying in Miami. Either Gamble himself or someone else attending these parties was preying on these people. The task force decided to invite themselves to the next party.

They put together a small group that would enter the party and plant a number of listening devices. They had sketches made of the members of The Order from Cloud's descriptions that were distributed to the police officers attending the party.

IN THE MEANTIME, IN NEW York, Banit had been sniffing around at Cloud's place. He noticed that his car had not moved out of his driveway for a few days. He decided to check it out. He stopped by the hardware store to buy the tools he would need to put his old craft to use. As he paid for the items, he could feel the anxiety flowing through him. *It's been a long time.* He then bought himself a mask and gloves along with clothing that he would need.

He waited until later that night. About midnight, he pulled his car up one block behind Cloud's house. He climbed the fence into Cloud's yard. Cloud had no alarms on his house. His windows were ideal for a burglary.

It took Banit less than three minutes to enter the house. He took a deep breath and began to move about. The house had a musty smell as if it had not been occupied for a while. He walked from the living room to the kitchen, where he opened up the refrigerator to find four cans of beer, a jar of mayonnaise, and some old Chinese food. From the kitchen he moved upstairs to the bedrooms and bathrooms. Inside a bathroom he noticed Cloud's toothbrush. It crossed his mind to piss on it before he left. One of the bedrooms had been converted into an office. On the walls were newspaper clippings of Banit's arrest and escape. Banit's picture was posted on a bulletin board along with sketches of Cat, James, Prince, and Ozzi. Banit pulled the chair from the desk, sat down, and began to look around the office. On the desk were a stack of papers compiled into various files. He pulled the chair closer to the desk, moved the stack of files in front of him, and began to go through them. *This creep is really working hard to bring us down.*

Banit discovered that Cat was in Miami and was still pulling off jux after jux. How he wished that he could be there with him on whatever jux he was on. *I have to get the news of Cloud being a cop to them somehow.*

James and Prince were back in Miami and ready for the next jux. This would be their last run, after which Prince planned to move to Jamaica. He had got his new passport. Plans were made for his mother to send his money to him bit by bit.

Cynthia had got back to Cat with her decision. She told him that she was with whatever he was going to do as long as he promised her that he would always be there for her. The plans were for them to move to England when he was done.

Gamble announced his arrangements to throw a few small parties leading up to the biggest party of the year and, quite possibly, the decade.

The task force made their way into the second of these parties to size up Gamble and to see if any of the members of the crew were present. After spotting Gamble, Cloud tried several times unsuccessfully throughout the night to approach him. As the party began to wind down, he realized he had another opportunity.

Gamble was sitting by the pool alone. He had a drink in his hand that he sipped slowly.

Cloud walked over to him. "This is an awesome party you put on here."

Gamble looked up at him. "Thanks."

"Pardon my manners, my name is Rick. You know, I flew in from Barbados two days ago just to attend this party. A friend of mine who had to leave early told me about it. I'll be back next week with a couple of my buddies, and I will certainly be back for the grand finale."

Money bells went off in Gamble's head, though Barbados sounded a bit too far. "Forgive me, but as you can see, I'm a bit tired from playing host all night. I do not mean to come off rude."

"Oh, I understand quite well. I wasn't trying to interrupt or rub you the wrong way. I simply want to congratulate you on a fabulous party."

"Thank you."

"Considering the marvelous job you've done here, would you mind helping me with a surprise party for a very special friend of mine?"

"I'm honored that you'd ask, but it's something I'd have to think about. You see, the grand-finale party in two weeks is my retirement. I'm stepping aside to let someone else become the king of Miami's party scene."

"Hmm, I see. Well, you did say that you would think about it, so I guess I'll approach you next week about it."

"That sounds great."

"Okay, I'll see you then. It was nice meeting you."

"Same here."

CLOUD WAS NOT 100 PERCENT sure, but he felt that he detected a slight Jamaican accent or some kind of Caribbean accent when he spoke with Gamble. If Gamble was the connection the task force was looking for, this would give the crew members something in common; something to make it easier for them to trust one another.

"But his paperwork says that he is an American," said Deputy Hemming.

"Yes, I know what it says. He could have Jamaican parents and could have spent some time there, anything is possible when it comes to these people. Either way I believe that something big is going to happen and that these parties are the backdrop for it. We need to get in the mix of it somehow. We need to act quickly, before we miss what's about to happen totally. We need a twenty-four-hour surveillance on this guy. We have to find the crew, we have to crash the party, and we have to do it all in two weeks," said Cloud.

Around-the-clock surveillance was placed on Gamble. His every move was watched. His phones were tapped. Gamble was under watchful eye for four days and he'd only left the house twice. Both times he went to the store. There was no sign of Cat, Prince, James, or Banit. Gamble's phone took no incoming calls. He made only one call, to a young lady to tell her about the party that coming weekend. It did not seem as though he was making any moves or preparations for anything outside of the ordinary party stuff. He was not moving as if he was up to anything or as if he was planning the biggest party of his life.

FOURTEEN

A round wooden table occupied the center of the room. On it sat the tools of the trade. Cat, Prince, and James were dressed in their ceremonial robes, each holding a gun in his right hand and the handbook of The Order in his left. In unison each rested his gun on top of his book and his hand on top of the gun and began their prayer.

"'The issue of this affair with us is we must keep a secret to the grave. No law, no amount of time, and no torturous devices must cause our tongues to betray this oath. Let not our thieving deeds one day cause us to be denied passage through the gates of heaven, because next to Christ were two thieves of which one was forgiven, so my heaven is guaranteed. In Christ we are The Order of Thieves,'" the crew recited together.

In a circle they then passed their guns and handbooks around to one another, until each man's gun and handbook came back to him.

"This is it, my brothers, the final run. After this we will part ways and most likely never see each other again. All good things come to an end, and we cannot continue forever, as it has already been proven. There is an old Jamaican saying that goes, 'Every day that bucket goes to the well, surely one day the bottom will drop out.' So it is best we get out while we are ahead and still can. We lost Ozzi, and Banit is no longer able to run with us. I don't know what happened to Cloud, but I'm sure it's not anything good. Whatever happened to him, I hope he is all right and in good health.

"The three of us are already rich, but in two weeks we will have more money than we could spend in our lifetimes. We have been blessed to have been placed in the company of one another. We have become experts of a craft that has opened doors beyond our wildest dreams. This is the craft of the jux. Even as we stand here together, there is a jux going down somewhere right now. There are many who practice, some will succeed and some won't.

"When that gun is flashed and a person is ordered to turn over his or her valuables, some will do so in respect of the jux, and some will resist and call the bluff. Not because they don't want to lose their possessions, but because they don't respect the jux. They don't think that the person holding the gun is going to cap their ass. You see, it's easy to pull your gun and order a person to turn over his goods. The willingness of those who would not hesitate to put some hot ones in a person for not respecting the jux has spread enough fear to make it easier for us; in essence that is not what we do. We don't always know what's waiting around the corner, but we operate on certain principles, and those ideals taught in your training allowed us to minimize disaster and optimize success. Cloud fucked up when he did not secure that target. He had something other than the jux on his mind. I've watched each one of you in the way you've applied the principles, and I can tell that you both have the jux on your mind at all times. You are true practitioners of our craft. I can say that if you were to stick up a dice game today, it would be done with greater efficiency and calculation than when you first joined The Order. That's because you, yourself, respect the jux! That is what this thing is about. Now we've been down here for a minute doing our thing, I'm sure that we have created a stir. Today I can surely say that somebody is looking into the jux we have committed, and they see the patterns. So today we're going to switch our MO to throw them off and to ensure our escape. By the time our victims realize that it's us, we'll be long gone. Now we have five more jux to take down before we're through. The targets were checked out thoroughly while you were away. From this, each of us will be able to walk away with at least seventy million dollars," said Cat passionately.

James and Prince looked at each other and smiled at the sound of that figure.

"I don't think I need to remind you how careful you need to be with that kind of money."

BANIT SAT IN HIS STOLEN car hoping to see James pull up. He needed to see him now more than ever. *How can I get to them and warn them?* He was becoming more and more frustrated, feeling like a sitting duck. Suddenly the thought to contact Cat's sister, Carroll, hit him. He started the car and pulled out of his parking space. Instead of calling or trying to get at her at her place of business, he would use his skills to gain entry into her home.

At 2 a.m., Banit pulled up one block behind Carroll's house and made his way through her backyard. He cased the house for a window to enter and found one open. Within thirty-five seconds he was on his knees in her kitchen waiting for his eyes to adjust to the darkness. He listened for a moment for any sounds. A phone was on the wall. He walked over and unplugged it. From there he quietly made his way through the house, checking all the ground-floor rooms. He decided to skip the basement and go right upstairs to the second floor where the bedrooms were.

None of the rooms were locked, they were all wide-open. The first room belonged to Carroll's daughter and the second to her son. The master bedroom was at the end of the hall. From one knee he looked into her bedroom at the two figures on the bed asleep. He slowly crept into the master bedroom and closed the door behind him. The door made a little squeak. He crept around to Carroll's side of the bed. He then rose up a bit and put his hand on her shoulder and gently shook her.

"Carroll," he called in a low voice.

She stirred a bit but did not wake.

"Carroll, wake up," Banit said, shaking her a little harder.

"What?" she responded in a half-conscious voice.

"Wake up, it's me, Banit."

She became more aware as she lifted her head from the pillow.

"It's Banit, Cat's friend. Don't be frightened or scream."

She now opened her eyes fully. Her vision became clearer as her eyes adjusted to his face. "Ahhhhh," she screamed out.

Banit quickly placed his hand over her mouth.

Carroll's husband jumped up at the sound of her scream. "What the fuck!?"

Banit looked over at him. "I'm a friend, I'm not here to harm you."

Carroll calmed down once she realized who he was. Banit removed his hand from her mouth. Her husband's limbs were frozen in fear.

"How did you get in here?"

"I came in through the kitchen window."

"You have one hell of a way of making an entry," she said as she caught her breath. "Why didn't you just knock on the front door?"

"I'm sure you know that you're still being watched, and I don't know if you know it or not, but I'm really hot since my escape from prison."

"Yeah, I remember it being all over the news." She began to get up out of the bed. "Come on, let's go downstairs where we can talk." She turned to her husband. "It's all right, honey, everything is fine."

She and Banit went downstairs and sat in the living room, on the couch, next to each other.

"First off, I'm sorry to come to your house

like this, but I've been trying to get word to Cat for the longest and I sorta ran out of options. I need to warn him of Cloud, and I didn't know where to turn or what to do, so I came here hoping you might still be in touch with him. Maybe you could get a message to him, let him know that Cloud was the one that brought us down. All that time he was a cop! I had no idea until he came to arrest me at Ozzi's wake."

"That's your friend who was killed in the shoot-out with the cops, right?"

"Yeah, he was my cousin. . . . Anyway, Cat needs to know that Cloud is hunting him and that he knows that they're in Miami. I broke into his house and came across a file that he had on us. Nigga needs to know that so Cloud can't sneak up on him."

"Well, I haven't been in touch with him. He ain't reached out to me ever since he went on the run. But, in the event that he does, I will let him know. Is there any way for me to reach you if he does contact me?"

Her question changed the tone of the conversation. He figured that she was playing it safe for Cat's safety, or why else would she ask him such a thing? "Well, I'm on the run from place to place."

"Okay then, I'm going to give you a number to a client of mine. She owns a boutique. I want you to call her once a week every Thursday. If I have any message for you, she will relay it to you for me. If anything new pops up for you, then you can do the same, and she will get word to me. If I need to see you, I will leave a message saying that the 'window is open.'"

Banit laughed.

"At least I'll be prepared the next time," she shot back.

Carroll did not tell Banit that Cat did stay in touch with her. They would contact each other every quarterly tax period. He would also send her money from his current jux for her to launder for him, as she had always done since he started juxing.

"We could bring Gamble in, but we have nothing on him," said one of the detectives on the task force. "We could raid the party, we know that there's going to be a lot of drugs there. We could put some or all of it on him and see if he would be willing to cooperate with us in bringing the rest in."

"That could work. It's an option, but what if he is not the link? What if it's someone else who frequents the parties for the purpose of picking out these people? Then we would have tipped our hat," said Deputy Hemming.

"You know, even though we have not seen

any signs of the crew or we haven't been able to link him to them, I still have a hunch that he is our man. There is just something about him. I can't quite put my finger on it, but I have this gut feeling about him. I think we should take our chances with the party, win or lose. If we happen to miss whatever it is, we can still keep watch on this guy and take him whenever we are ready. I'm sure if he is connected to them, there will be a slipup somewhere along the line. In the meantime, I think we should set up a few detectives to sniff out any other possible links, anything that we might be overlooking. We are sure that whoever the link is, he or she will be at those parties. Everybody needs to get in the party this time. We need to put on our best aristocratic attires and performances; pull out the best cards in the pound. I already have a rapport with him, so I'll be able to get close to him. I'll be trying to see what he is looking at all night," Cloud continued. "One more thing. We need to find the finest female officer on the force and dress her up for the occasion. I'm going to use her as my date and as leverage. She might be able to spend more time with him than I can."

"That would have to be Tina, hands down," replied another officer. "She works downstairs in evidence."

"In evidence?" asked Cloud.

"Yeah."

"Well, does she know anything about working the field?"

"Yeah, she is one of our best."

"So why'd she stop?"

"She got burned out and needed a break."

"Well, then I think you need to pull her and bring her up to speed on everything. As a backup, we also need to get some cameras in there. Get some of the drug usage on tape, especially some of those models and actors using this stuff. You never know, it might come in handy later."

"It sounds good," said the sheriff, who was sitting in.

"Okay then, people, let's get to work!"

TEN P.M. AND THE PARTY was under way. The valet was busy parking the hottest cars from BMWs to Porsches to Rovers. Everyone was dressed to impress. Miami's elite social crowd was in full attendance. Cloud and Tina, who was going by the name Shary, pulled up in a Maserati. When they entered the mansion, Cloud and Tina set out to find Gamble. They walked around for forty-five minutes looking for him.

"Where the hell is he?" asked Cloud.

Cloud spotted Deputy Hemming and motioned him over. "I haven't seen Gamble anywhere. What about you?"

"No, I haven't seen him either."

"Check with the others and get back to me."

"Will do."

"Come on, let's take another spin," Cloud said to Tina.

They walked around again, covering the entire place, and still no sign of Gamble. Cloud motioned Hemming over again. "Anything?"

"Still no signs of him, but I must say the party is definitely on its way even without him. We are getting some great shots of the powder room."

"Good, tell them to keep rolling and get as much as they can. Let's try to find out who brought the drugs in here."

They split up. Cloud and Tina went off and began to mingle with the guests to see if anyone might know where the hell Gamble was. About an hour later, a loud uproar, clapping and whistling, came from the mansion's entrance. Tina and Cloud made their way through the crowd to see what all the excitement was about. There he was, Gamble. He made quite an entrance. The crowd was hailing him as the man of the hour. The party king had arrived. They cheered and patted him on the back as he walked by. He walked to the back of the house to the pool and DJ booth. He grabbed the microphone. He gave the DJ a nod, which brought the music to a halt.

Everyone turned his or her attention to Gamble. Those who could make their way through the house to the back by the pool did so. Those who could not simply stood where they were and listened to him through the speakers.

"How y'all feeling out there?" he screamed into the microphone.

The crowd responded in an eruption of loud cheers. Gamble listened until it subsided.

"That's what I'm talking about. I want to thank you all for coming out and enjoying yourself with me. It's been a long time since my humble beginnings in this great city of ours. For years you all have supported me. You made me what I am today. Without all of you there would be no me. You have followed me from one club to another, and when they shut me down, you followed me to my doorsteps. I feel very blessed to look out and see all of you, to see many of the same faces that I've seen for years. It's been an honor to be at your service for so long."

A young lady from the crowd screamed, "We love you, Gamble!"

Gamble held his head down and smiled. "Thank you, I love you, too. That is why this transition will be such a difficult feat for me. As you all know, I am bringing my show to a close."

Moans of disappointment passed through his audience.

"I know, I know, it's sad. I feel the same way."

"Don't leave us, Gamble!" someone screamed from the crowd.

"Thank you, I appreciate it, really, I do, but it's time to pack it up. So in celebration of all the good times we've had together, all the dance floors we've rocked, and all the records we've grooved to, we are going to do it one last time. We are going to rock Miami down to its knees with the biggest, loudest, and wildest party this city has ever seen!"

The crowd went crazy cheering.

"Well, starting next Friday, we are going to party all the way till Monday."

The crowd was now in a frenzy. Gamble gave the microphone back to the DJ, who started the music again. The man of the hour began to mingle with his people.

Cloud and Tina watched him from a distance. "Let's give him some time to settle in before we approach him," said Cloud. "I don't want to run the risk of being brushed off and considered to be an annoyance for the rest of the night. There's a lot of important people that I'm sure he would like to mingle with first."

"How could you ever be considered an annoyance with me standing at your side?"

Cloud looked at her from head to toe and smiled. "You're absolutely right."

"He'll be too busy thinking about fucking me."

"That's true, but this guy might be a queer for all we know."

"Nah, he's no queer."

"How do you know that?"

"It's just something a woman knows and can tell you about a man."

"I see. Well, let's check in with the others and see if they've spotted anything unusual."

They walked around until they found Hemming.

"So how are things going on your end?"

"Good so far, I believe we have pinpointed who is responsible for the drugs here. We have also linked him with our man. Earlier when he came in, he stopped and had a quick chat with him."

"Great, so at least we have something to work with." Cloud then turned to Tina. "Well, darling, are you ready?"

"Let's go."

They walked off in search of Gamble. Up the steps and around the corner then down the hall to the balcony, where he was overlooking the crowd, making sure that all were enjoying themselves. They located him with his back turned to them, looking over the railing. They walked out onto the balcony.

"There he is!" Cloud said in a loud enough voice for him to hear. Gamble turned around and smiled, recognizing Cloud from the previous party. Cloud held out his hand to shake Gamble's, who returned the gesture.

"The man of the hour!"

"Wait, don't tell me," said Gamble. "Rick, is it?"

"You got it."

"How are you doing?"

"I'm doing great, having a ball."

"That's fabulous, I'm glad you could make it."

"I wouldn't have missed it for the world. You did it again, friend. I can't wait until next week to see you outdo this," Cloud said.

"Well, it's not me that usually clinches a party, it's the people that usually outdo it. I just provide the stage and the atmosphere for them to feel comfortable in losing themselves. Just letting go and getting wild, doing things they never saw themselves doing before and loving it."

"You know, it's almost poetry the way you put it."

"That's a first, I've never heard that one before."

"Well, anyway, I've brought along someone that I would like you to meet." Cloud stepped aside and motioned Tina to step forward. "This is a good friend of mine, Shary. I told her all about you and your last party, how much of a blast I had. She's been dying to meet you ever since. She told me that she would kill me if I didn't bring her along on this one."

Gamble took her hand and looked her up and down. He looked her in her eyes. For a second he was almost speechless. She was gorgeous. Cloud noticed the effect she was having on him.

"Shary, it is my pleasure to meet such a beautiful lady." Gamble leaned forward and kissed her hand.

"Why, thank you, and likewise to meet such a man. Your party is everything and more."

"Is the party the only thing that has met your expectations so far?"

"Well, the night is still young. Why don't you give me some time to get back to you on that one."

"Fair enough. In that case I'm forced to be your personal host for the rest of the night, that is, if my good friend Rick here doesn't mind."

"No, not at all, be my guest," replied Cloud. "In fact, I'll leave you two alone for a while." He walked off and headed back down the stairs.

"I want to make sure that everything goes beyond your expectations tonight, so I'm not letting you out of my sight."

"That sounds like an offer I can't refuse."

Cloud spotted Hemming by the bar and walked over to him. "Hey, buddy, anything new?"

"Not much, things are pretty much the same here. We've got our eyes peeled. So how did things go with Tina? Were you able to drop her off on him?"

"It worked like a charm, and she's really working that sucker. You should have seen the way he fell for her. That girl needs to get back in the field, she is totally cut out for it."

"That's good to hear, she's one of the good ones we have on the force."

"Well, it doesn't look like the rest of the crew are going to show up here tonight. I do think they'll be at the next and supposedly the final party. In the meantime, I'm going to snoop around and try to work some angles myself. Who knows, I might find me a rich chick who wants to marry me." They both laughed.

THE PARTY WAS ABOUT TO come to a close for the night. The task force had enough on tape to send the tabloids into a frenzy. Gamble and Tina were still chatting up a storm.

Cloud approached them. "Well, I see that you don't look as tired tonight as you did last week."

"I have Shary to thank for keeping me energized and alive all night."

"So I take it that my friend has been good to you?"

"She has been a wonderful companion."

"That's good to hear. I'm glad I was able to introduce the both of you."

"So am I. Ms. Shary, has the party and environment surpassed your expectations?" Gamble asked.

"Oh, absolutely. You have been the best host. I can see why you're so loved here."

"Thank you. I guess that means I will see you again for the grand finale?"

"Death couldn't keep me away."

"Then I will be looking forward to seeing you again. My guess is you have come to scoop her away for your departure, so I won't keep you any longer than I need to. Rick, it's been a pleasure meeting you. I think I might be able to fly down to Barbados and take care of that little business of yours once this is all over."

"That is just fabulous. She must've really had an effect on you."

Gamble leaned over and whispered into his ear, "Was that not her purpose?"

Cloud and Tina said their good-byes and left the party.

FIFTEEN

Banit switched his car after visiting Carroll. With nothing much to do while he waited to hear from her, he decided to go out and buy himself some clothes. He wanted a break from feeling like a wanted man.

He pulled up and parked the car in the Queens Center Mall's parking lot. He got out and went through the different stores looking for some clothes. As he was walking through the mall, a young lady caught his eye. *She has a great set of tits. Yeah, that's exactly what I need, some pussy. I ain't had no pussy since I went to the joint.*

He came upon a jewelry store as he was walking. He strolled in and looked around the showcases.

"Sir, can I help you with anything?" a young saleslady asked.

"I don't know yet. I wanna treat myself to some bling."

"Maybe I can give you a hand. Right over here we have a nice selection of watches, rings, and chains. You might find something to your liking."

She pointed Banit to his left to the other end of the showcase. "Here we have some nice *affordable* pieces," she stressed.

Banit looked down through the glass at the jewelry. He noticed that it looked cheap. *I can't pick nobody up with those!*

"Nah, I don't like none of this stuff. How about we go back over there. I think I saw something that I liked."

"But you haven't even looked over the selection."

"I've seen enough. I have asked you to show me the ones back down there," he said sternly.

She raised her eyebrows. They walked back down to the other end.

"That one right there with the yellow-looking diamond."

"That is one of our more expensive pieces. It is a princess-cut."

"Is that right?"

"That's right."

"Good, then I'll take it along with that chain

next to it, and that bracelet right there. I also want to take a look at your watches."

"And how will you be paying?"

"Cash. Greenbacks or whatever you want to call it."

"You do realize that you are looking at about twenty thousand dollars so far?" she said sarcastically.

"Is that all? No need to wrap it up, I'll be wearing it home."

She took the pieces out of the showcase, then walked down to where he was standing looking at the watches. Her attitude had become more cordial.

"I like that one there."

"That is an excellent choice. That, my friend, is one of our best brands—Vacheron Constantin." She smiled.

"I'll take it."

"Okay then, let me get that out for you and wrap it up."

"I said I'll be wearing it home."

"Oh, that's right, my apologies." She smiled again.

Banit noticed her beauty for the first time. He smiled at her as her smile grew brighter.

"While you're at it, why don't you pick up something for yourself, as well," he said, staring deeply into her blue eyes.

She was at a loss for words for a few seconds. "I'm sorry, but I'm not allowed to do that, thank you anyway. You're very kind."

"What is it, job policies?"

"Yes, it's not considered appropriate."

"Appropriate? Who cares about appropriate?"

"I'm sorry, but I can't. I may be out of a job if I accept anything from a customer."

"Okay then, tell you what. Why don't you pick something out that you like, or better yet, why don't you select something for me that you find appropriate for a lady friend."

She moved her long blond hair from the side of her face and smiled. "What exactly is the style of your lady friend?"

"I don't know, I'll judge her from your selection."

She began to blush, hardly able to look Banit in his face. "How about that one?" She pointed to the lady's watch that matched Banit's.

He smiled. "Yes, she is very special. Wrap that one up for me."

He then went into his bag and pulled out a stack of cash and placed it on the counter. "Count out the amount from there."

She looked up at him with a surprised look on her face. He picked up his jewelry and went to the mirror while she nervously counted the cash. When she was finished, he returned to the counter.

"All done? So what time do you blow this joint?"

She didn't hesitate as she looked at the watch he'd purchased for her. "In two hours."

"See you then," Banit said, turning to leave the store.

"Wait, what's your name?"

"What's yours?" he shot back.

"Gabrielle."

"I'll see you in two hours, Gabrielle. I'll be outside waiting."

"Okay then," she said, smiling.

Two hours later she walked out the front door of the mall to a waiting car. Her eyes raised when she saw the S-Type Jaguar. She stepped off the sidewalk and opened the door.

"That was the longest two hours I ever had to wait."

She smiled big, then asked, "So what do you want to do?"

"I don't know, whatever you want to do."

"You're leaving it all to me?"

"I guess so."

"Well, that sounds good."

"You should open the glove compartment."

She did as he said and inside was the watch. She reached in and took it out.

"You know, I didn't think you were serious until I saw you parked out here."

"Well, as you can see, I'm very serious. You are the special friend," he said, placing the watch on her wrist. "I'm glad you like it."

"I should like it, after all I picked it."

"Yes, you did, and a good choice I might add."

Banit had only one thing on his mind—sex.

"I bet a man like you gets whatever he wants," she said teasingly.

"Well, not exactly. You would be surprised to know how hard I have to work for the things I want."

"Oh, really?"

"What? You don't believe that I have to work very hard for the things I want?" he asked, smiling.

He sensed that he did not have to wine and dine her, so he got on the highway and headed for La Guardia Airport. He pulled into the parking lot of the Red Inn Hotel. He and Gabrielle checked in. Banit decided that he was going to take his time and enjoy himself. They went into the hotel bar and had a couple of drinks. After about an hour at the bar, they got onto the elevator and went up to their room.

They were both tipsy and ended up in the shower caressing and kissing each other. The hot water felt good on his body, waking him up a little bit. She got down on her knees and took his dick in her mouth. She sucked it slow with long strokes in and out of her mouth, deep-throating it. *This bitch definitely knows what she's doing.* She looked up into his eyes as she slurped it in and out.

"It tastes good, baby. I want you to cum down my throat."

"Bitch, you a freak, huh?"

She picked up her pace, swallowing her excess saliva. He could feel himself reaching his climax. He wanted to hold on and not cum so soon, but after going without sex for so long, he couldn't control himself.

"Ahhh, it's coming. Fuck, I'm about to bust off. Swallow it, swallow it, baby," he shouted as he put his hands against the wall to brace himself.

"Ummm, umm."

"Yeah, I'm cumming for you, right in your mouth, baby." He let out a loud sigh of relief as he ejaculated in her mouth. She sucked and swallowed every drop of it.

They then moved to the bed, where he turned on the TV and ordered a movie. The movie watching did not last for long. She put her hand between his legs and began to rub his dick until it slowly began to get erect again. She then moved down to his waist and took it into her mouth again. She sucked it until he was hard as a rock.

Damn, this bitch is a freak for real.

She then got up on top of him. She began to rub the head of his dick between the folds of her pussy, then slowly guided it into her hole. Once she got it in halfway, she let it go and lowered herself onto it.

"Turn around, I want to see your ass bounce up and down on that."

She laughed, then did what he asked.

"Yeah, that's how I like it."

He put his hands on her ass and began to massage it as she rode his cock up and down. After a while they switched positions and she got on her hands and knees. He pounded her until she screamed like a wild animal. He turned her around onto her back. He spread her legs wide, on either side of her head, then penetrated her.

"Look at it while you fuck it," she said.

He began to slam into her, his balls slapping against her ass.

"Yes, fuck me, fuck me harder! I want you to hurt me."

After pounding away at her for a while he told her to turn around. She got on her hands and knees again. He pulled her to the edge of the bed as he stood on the floor and guided himself into her. He held her by the waist, then began a ferocious assault, pounding away at her pussy from behind. From there he took her through a series of positions, twisting and stretching her in every direction.

Later that night Banit awoke to see her fast asleep. He quietly got out of the bed. He got dressed, making sure he made no sound that might awaken her. He then got his jewelry together and placed the pieces in his pockets. He also took the time to pick up the watch he'd bought for her and put it into his pocket. He stood over her and looked at her naked body lying on the bed one last time before leaving her.

The next day he stopped off at another jewelry store and resold all the jewelry that he'd bought. After that, he dialed the number that Carroll had given him, leaving a message that he needed to see her. A day later, he called back to get her response.

BANIT CLIMBED THROUGH THE KITCHEN window at Carroll's house. From the kitchen he walked into the living room. He wasn't nervous entering the house this time. When he got into the living room, he saw a figure sitting on the couch. He stopped in his tracks.

"Come on in, it's me," she said. "I've been

waiting on you for the past two hours. I didn't know what time you would arrive."

He walked over and sat next to her on the couch.

"How you doing?" she asked.

"I'm fine, considering."

"I know, I can't even imagine all that you are going through. Well, I have some good news for you. I made contact with Cat."

Banit's eyes widened. "You did?"

"Yes, I did."

"Tell me, what he said? Did you tell him that you was in touch with me?"

"Well, I did not talk to him directly, but he did get my message. I sent everything that you told me. He sent word back that he got it. That was all, he didn't say anything else. So, what do you plan to do now?"

"I don't know, I guess it's time for me to move on now. My job is done. There is nothing else that I can do," Banit said with a sad look on his face.

"Well, whatever you do, you make sure that you take care of yourself."

He looked at her. "Thank you. I will. When I get settled, I will send you word on where I'm at. You could give that to Cat so he could get up with me if he wants to or if he needs anything."

"Fine, just be very careful out there."

SIXTEEN

Gamble pulled his visor down to retrieve his registration and insurance cards. He then went into his wallet and got his license out and handed them to the trooper.

"If you don't mind me asking, sir, for what reason was I stopped?"

"We are conducting a routine traffic stop in this area of the highway."

"Oh, I see."

Gamble noticed that the trooper's eyes were busy looking all over his car. The trooper walked back to his car to radio in his stop to the task force. He returned to Gamble's car and gave him back his license and told him to have a nice day.

Gamble smiled as he drove off, looking at the trooper in his mirror. "Stupid fucks!"

• • •

Cloud's flight was just off the Miami runway. After arriving in New York at 2 p.m., he went home to drop off his things, then to the precinct to file his report. Cloud sat at his desk typing up the report for his boss. When he was done, he dropped it off on the chief's desk. He then began to kick it around the office, telling everybody how beautiful Florida was. He was due back in Miami the next day for the grand-finale party.

After leaving the precinct, he stopped off at a diner and got something to eat. He spent about an hour there hanging with his buddies. He got home at about seven thirty in the evening, put his things down, and went to take a shower. He then went into his home office to look over some paperwork. He sat at the desk and began to go through the files. He flipped through the first couple of pages before he noticed that some of the papers were out of order. He put them back into their original order. He left his office and went into his bedroom. He loved watching reruns of *Kojak*, a seventies TV show about a detective who always got his man. He opened his DVD case and began to go through the selections. He pulled one out and popped it into the DVD player, then lay back and stretched out on his bed, pressing play on the remote control. He watched until his eyes began to get tired and he fell asleep.

BACK AT THE PRECINCT

"ARE YOU SURE?"

"Yes, sir."

"And you are saying that the caller did not leave a name?" asked Andrews, Cloud's boss. He put his hand on his chin and began to think about the situation. "I find this hard to believe." He shook his head. "This is not making any sense at all. Why would he do such a thing?"

The detective who took the call hesitated at first, then decided to go ahead and say what was on his mind. "Well, there is the factor of money. The caller did say he was paid a quarter million dollars and drugs."

"Damn that son of a bitch!" yelled Andrews as he slammed his fist into his desk. "If this is true, I'm going to make sure that he gets buried under some jail for the rest of his natural life." Shaking his head, he said, "He's going to be sorry for making me look like a damn fool!"

Andrews emerged from behind his desk and grabbed his hat from the coatrack. "Call the captain and tell him to meet me in the situation room," he told the detective.

In the situation room, Commander Andrews

and the captain went over what the caller had said. They decided that they would act on the information given. They came up with a plan on how to turn what was a potentially bad public relations situation into a good one.

"I'll call Special Ops while you give the media a call," said the captain.

Andrews nodded and began walking toward the door. He stopped suddenly and looked directly at the captain. "Tell the boys to be careful on this one. After all, he is a cop and we don't know just how true this is."

"Don't worry, I'll do that. In fact, just to make sure that everything is done by the book, I am going to personally supervise this one."

"Thank you, sir."

"No problem."

Andrews turned and reached for the door handle still hoping that what he heard wasn't true—that it was a prank call.

"Andrews!" called the captain.

The commander turned around in response.

"Look, these things do happen sometimes. It's always sad when it happens to one of your own. You shouldn't beat yourself up too much over it."

"I understand, sir."

THE TASK FORCE HAD SET up a police line to keep the media cameras back and out of the range of their operational field. The Special Ops truck pulled up on the block with seven more cars of supporting officers. The captain and Andrews pulled up in their car and parked across the street. The commander of the team got out of the truck and walked over to the captain as he and Andrews got out of their vehicle.

"Remember, everything by the book! I want it surgical and clean, you got that?" the captain asked his commander clearly and crisply.

"Yes, sir. Loud and clear."

"All right, then you can send your men in now."

"Affirmative, sir." The commander walked back to the truck to inform his unit they were about to storm the house.

"What the fuck!" exclaimed Cloud as he jumped out of his sleep at the sound of the loud crash. He quickly got out of his bed and reached for his gun on the dresser, then raced out into the hallway. He was quickly bombarded by tear gas, which engulfed the hallway. He pulled his T-shirt over his nose and mouth and began to make his way to the stairs, gun in hand. As he got to the steps, he heard a voice yell out, "Police! Freeze!"

"Hold your fire, I'm a cop."

With his hands and gun in the air Cloud looked and saw the men dressed in SWAT uniforms with their guns aimed at him.

"Drop the gun and get down on the floor now!"

"Don't shoot, I'm a cop!"

"Get down now!"

Cloud slowly put his gun down on the floor. "Okay, okay, just don't shoot, I'm a cop!"

He turned around and slowly lay down on his stomach. In no time the officers were up the stairs and on top of him. As they put the handcuffs on him, he kept telling them he was a cop. They lifted him off the floor and walked him outside, where they laid him on the lawn, in his front yard. More cops went into the house to conduct a search. Ten minutes later they came out again with another man in cuffs. They walked him over and laid him on the lawn a few feet from Cloud's left. Cloud looked over to his left and could not believe his eyes.

"Motherfucker!" he shouted. "What the fuck are you doing here!"

"Hey, old friend. How you been?" said Banit with a smile.

"What you doing here?"

"I missed you, so I thought that I would give my old friend a visit."

The officers then walked out of the house with two duffel bags. They walked down the pathway to the captain's car, where they placed the bags on the hood of the car.

The captain unzipped them. "Damn!"

By the look on the captain's face, Andrews knew his worst fears had come true. He looked into the bags and saw the money and drugs: $250,000 in cash, ten kilos of cocaine, and seven illegal handguns. He just shook his head in disgust.

The captain gave a nod to the commander, who then put his radio to his mouth. "Go ahead, let them through."

The officers who were guarding the police lines dropped the tape, and reporters and cameramen and camerawomen went running down the block to the scene. Suddenly the police floodlights turned onto Banit and Cloud lying on the grass as the reporters got to them and began snapping away. Cloud then heard the voices of the reporters yelling questions at him:

"Why did you do it?"

"How much money did he pay you?"

"What were you planning to do with the drugs?"

Banit began to laugh in Cloud's face.

"What the fuck is so funny?"

"Your expression. Ha, ha, ha. You should see the look on your face."

"You got something to do with this?" Cloud demanded.

"Ha, ha, ha. Welcome to Hollywood, my friend."

"What the fuck did you do?"

"What the fuck did *I* do? No, no, no, you mean what the fuck did you do? You see, my good friend, you didn't respect the jux. But don't worry, you will after all of this is over. Ha, ha, ha . . ." Banit's laughter echoed into the night as the cameras flashed.

The officers picked them both up off the ground and began to escort them to separate cars. Flashbulbs were going off and more questions were being thrown at them as they walked by the reporters. Across the street, Cloud saw Andrews and the captain standing together. He shouted out to them, but they acted as if they couldn't hear him. He was placed in the back of the squad car.

"Sir, I'm being set up. I don't know what's going on!" said Cloud to Andrews.

"In all my years, this is a first. I just want to know, how could you do it and live with yourself? How could you wake up every day and go to work pretending to be a cop? How do you pretend to be something you're not for so long?" responded Andrews.

"I'm telling you, sir, I know nothing of this."

"Well, for your sake, you better know what's going on and fast, because you're in a shitload of trouble, and I don't think even God could help you out of this mess."

"Please, sir, you gotta believe that I don't have anything to do with this!"

"Stop! The insanity plea isn't gonna work for you! Just face it. You got caught."

"I'm telling you, sir!"

Andrews turned to the driver. "I've heard enough of this. Get this trash out of here! Now!"

The following day it was all over the news: CROOKED COP HELPS PRISONER ESCAPE FROM JAIL.

THE NEWS OF CLOUD'S ARREST had reached the task force in Miami. Their investigation into The Order of Thieves had been severely compromised. They were no longer sure if what they had and who they were looking at were in fact the brotherhood. Cloud could have been leading them down the wrong path all this time to keep them off the real brotherhood's trail.

It was two hours before the party. The task force was not certain of their next move.

"We know one thing for sure: there are illegal activities going on in these parties and tonight will be no exception. We are sure that there will be lots of drugs in there tonight, so if all else fails, we can grab hold of this Gamble guy and his friend Bull," Deputy Hemming said.

They assembled the team, including Tina,

and geared up for the party. All the officers designated to enter the party were decked out to the fullest.

Tina flaunted a turquoise peekaboo bodice with a long, flowing overcoat. She was a stunner, the perfect blend of a good girl meets the sexpot. Without Cloud, she deliberately chose this sexy, revealing dress that she hoped would captivate Gamble all night and keep him distracted. She planned to tell him that Cloud had got really sick and was unable to attend. She knew that she would have an advantage with Gamble's thinking that he had her to himself for the entire weekend.

SEVENTEEN

Less than a day to go before the party, the decorators and caterers were busy getting everything ready. Gamble was going over the catering and checking out the sound system. He and the DJ were reviewing the music selections to make sure that the best joints were played. Later on in the evening, his friend Bull stopped by. He had a duffel bag with him when he got out of his car. Gamble headed downstairs to meet him.

"Yes, my yute, what going on, brethren?" said Bull as he and Gamble embraced each other.

"Me trying to make sure that everything goes well tomorrow."

"Yes, me see dat everything is coming along really well. It's going to be sad when it's all over."

"It's never going to be over. They gonna still have you to carry it on once I'm gone," said Gamble.

"I hear dat, but can't nobody do it like you, mon."

Gamble laughed. "Don't worry, you'll get the hang of it. So, was you able to get the Xanax?"

"Come on, mon, what's my name? You know I got you, dog."

They walked farther into the house.

"So is that cousin of yours going to be there at the party, too?" Bull asked Gamble.

Gamble laughed again. "Oh, so you like my cousin I see."

"I've been checking her out, but I felt funny asking you what's up with her, 'cause I don't know how you might take it. But since this is your last party before you break out, I don't know if I'm going to see her again. I'm thinking that I better take my chances and ask you now before it's too late."

Gamble shook his head, then turned to him. "My friend, sorry to bust your bubble, but she is already taken."

"Damn! Say it ain't so."

"I'm afraid that it is."

"Damn, I missed another one by moving too late."

They walked to the back and into the powder room. There Bull began to set up for the next day. Bull opened up the rear compartment of the duffel bag that held the narcotics for the party. He pulled out a little pouch and handed it to Gamble. "Here you go."

"Good looking out."

"Mon, I told you that it ain't nothing."

Gamble opened the pouch and peeped inside. He took out one of the pills, then put it back into the pouch.

"We need to be extra careful tonight. I saw on the news that one of the men from the last party was an undercover cop. He was arrested for being involved in some illegal shit. I'm not sure if he has friends that might show up," Gamble warned as he left Bull to finish setting up.

Gamble walked out of the house and around the side toward the garage. He came to the door that he had specially built. He looked around to see if anybody was paying attention to him. The workmen were busy stringing up the lights around the house. They were not paying Gamble any mind. He opened the door and went into the garage.

Gamble pulled out all the stops for the grand finale. It was not just a party, but a show. It got under way around midnight. At 12:10 a.m. exactly, the fireworks went off. All the colors of the rainbow lit the night sky for miles. Following the fireworks, the caterers pulled the cover off the pool, releasing three thousand helium-filled balloons into the air. Another ten seconds of fireworks went off after that. Next, a hot-air balloon appeared in the sky over the backyard and slowly lowered itself onto the lawn. Several of Gamble's employees ran over to secure it. Suddenly the music came on as male and female exotic dancers climbed out of the balloon basket.

Outside, Hemming and his team approached the gate, where they were met by security.

"I'm sorry, sir, but I can't let you in there without an invitation," said the big man.

"But I'm a friend of the host," said Hemming.

"I understand that, sir, but if your name isn't on the guest list, I can't let you in there."

"Ah, come on, this is the biggest party of the year! You have to let me in."

The man shook his head no. "I'm sorry but I can't."

By this time the rest of the team were standing behind him and overheard the conversation.

"Could you please step aside and let these people through so I can check their names against my list?"

Hemming could not believe that they had come this far only to be turned back.

"How about a crisp fifty-dollar bill?" asked

Hemming as he went into his pocket and pulled out his wallet.

"I'm really sorry, sir, but that's not going to happen. Now, if you don't mind, could you please step aside and let me do my job?"

Hemming, Tina, and the rest of the team receded.

"What we need is a warrant to get in there," said Tina.

"Yeah, but where are we going to get one from at this time of the night?" asked Hemming.

"Wait a minute, we just might be in some luck. There is a judge who is a very good friend of our captain. We were able to use him once before to get a late-night warrant to go in on a couple of drug runners. If I could get to the captain, we might be able to get to that judge."

Gamble was the last to step out of the hot-air balloon basket. The crowd went into an uproar when they saw him. After making his way through the crowd and greeting those who came up to him, he went upstairs to the balcony overlooking the crowd, as he usually did.

A security person came and whispered something into his ear. After that, both of them went into a private room upstairs. The guard told him that the cops had showed up just as

Gamble knew they were going to, as undercovers, and that they were turned away at the gate. Gamble smiled and patted the guard on the back, then both of them left the room.

The guard went back to his job and Gamble went back to the balcony to play host, looking over the many partygoers enjoying themselves. He spent another half hour on the balcony, then went to the refreshment table and told one of the caterers to fix him up a tray of Moët glasses. Gamble took the tray with the glasses and walked out to the backyard. He walked around as if he was looking for someone in particular.

"There you go!" said Gamble as he approached Vito.

The young Italian man turned and saw Gamble and his face lit up. "Hey, how are you, good friend?" he replied in his Italian accent.

"I'm fine, just trying to be a good host to my good friend, that's all."

"You never stop being humble even though you are the man of the hour. I like that about you. My father could use a good man like you, Gamble."

"That is kind of you, I will definitely think it over, it sounds good." Gamble rolled his eyes so that Vito could not see him.

"It is. You could make a lot of money for yourself."

"Now you're talking my language," Gamble

said with a smirk. "Would you like to drink with me while we walk and talk about this possible job?"

"Sure, why not?" asked Vito as he took one of the glasses from the tray. He sipped on his Moët as they made their way through the crowd of people. They walked through the house and came out a side door. They were now at the top of the driveway where few people were around.

"Oh, by the way, there is something that I would like to show you," Gamble said.

When they got to the side door of the garage, Gamble opened it and showed him in. He walked in behind Vito and closed the door. Ten minutes later, Gamble walked out alone to rejoin the party. With the tray of drinks in his hand, he entered the house and made his way through the crowd. As he was walking through the living room, he suddenly stopped and took a couple of steps back. He turned and began to walk over to the left side of the room.

"Lydia, I've been looking all over for you, where have you been, girl?"

"Oh, I've just been having a ball since the party started, are you kidding me?"

"That's just fabulous to hear."

"Gamble, you are definitely the man." She rested her hand on his shoulder and looked into his eyes with a seductive stare.

"Care to take a walk with me? Here, have a drink with me." He handed her a glass.

"Are you for real? Gamble, I'll walk with you anywhere."

She was all over him. Both of them walked the same route that he and Vito walked only moments earlier. As they approached the garage door, the desire to fuck her crept into Gamble's mind. He was looking at her perfect ass as she walked up the driveway at the side of the house. When they got to the side door of the garage, he stopped and looked down at her. He grabbed her by the hand.

"Come with me."

They went behind the garage, where Gamble placed the tray down on the ground. He then leaned her back against the wall as they stared into each other's eyes. His gaze lowered to her lips, then he leaned forward and began to kiss her really hard. Their hands were all over each other. He ran his hands up her skirt and into her panties, where he began to rub her pussy lips. She was wet and warm. She pulled him close to her and unfastened his belt. With his pants down to his ankles he turned her around and pulled her dress up. He then gathered her panties to the side. Gamble's cock was rock hard. He began to rub his dick against the crack of her ass. With his left hand braced against the wall and his right gripping her waist, he slammed his cock deep into her pussy. She let out a short scream. Slowly he began to pick up speed, thrusting into her harder and harder. She screamed even louder, but the loud music muffled her cries.

"I'm feeling dizzy, Gamble!" she said as he banged away at her.

"Shit! Just hold on, baby, I'm cumming right now!" He pumped away faster and faster trying to cum before she passed out. He felt it building up, he was about to explode. He struggled to hold her up while he pumped out his cum into her. Her body suddenly went limp in his hands as she passed out from the Xanax that he had put into her glass of Moët.

When he was done, he rested her on the ground while he pulled his pants back up and straightened his clothes. He then lifted her up over his shoulders and quickly took her into the garage. Seconds later, he came back out and went to pick up the tray of drinks and rejoined the party.

THE CAPTAIN AND HEMMING SAT in the judge's lounge waiting to be called into his study. Several minutes later they were summoned in.

"Hello, Brian," said the judge as he greeted the captain.

"How are you, Judge James?"

"I'm doing fine, just fine. It's been a while since I've seen you."

"What? Something like two years?" said the captain.

"I don't know, I haven't been keeping track. So how is that golf game of yours? Have you been working on that swing?"

"To tell you the truth I haven't been able to get out much lately. So I don't know what my swing looks like these days."

The judge put his hand on the captain's shoulder and laughed. "That's too bad. I know what you mean about not being able to get out much. I haven't been out there in about four months. My calendar has been booked up for the past six months and I don't see any break in sight. Anyway, tell me, what brings you to my home at this time of the night?"

The captain introduced Hemming to the judge, then let him explain the case and the problems that they were having. When the judge heard that the thieves were preying on wealthy people, he became interested.

"So you see, Judge, without a warrant, it is quite possible that we'll lose this case."

"I see. So, you say you have enough evidence to support a warrant?"

"Yes, sir. And if we get in there, we will surely have a lot more."

The judge got up and went to his desk and pulled out a warrant form and began to fill it out.

"I'm just curious as to who might be some of the people at this party?"

"This is the type of party that attracts the elite socialites in Florida."

"When you say the elite, do you mean people like representatives of civil-liberties groups, lawyers, senators, or Hollywood affiliates?"

"It is quite possible that some or all of those people would be there. It's a party of the rich, and, yes, the powerful."

The judge stopped writing and put his pen down on his desk. "I don't know about this one, Brian." The judge shook his head.

"Why is that, sir?"

"This sounds like a PR disaster waiting to happen. And as you know, this is an election year. I just wouldn't be able to afford some big-shot lawyer up in arms making any trouble for me as the judge who issues such a warrant."

"Sir, I don't think that things would go that far."

"That's just it, you cannot guarantee anything. You know how people with money get when they feel their rights have been violated. I'm sorry, boys, I don't think that I'm going to be able to help you out on this one."

"Please, sir, we really need your help," pleaded the captain.

"I would love to help you out, but I just can't chance it. The governor would be on my ass if there was to be any kind of backlash from this, because it would surely reflect on him for putting me on the bench."

Lydia, who was ripping off the pharmaceutical companies, and Vito, whose father was the biggest drug lord in Florida, woke up from their sleep along with four other people. They were tied and bound. Cat, James, and Prince were standing around them dressed in black tuxedos, masks, and gloves.

"Hello, ladies and gentlemen. I know you are all frightened and confused as to what's going on right now. But don't worry, as long as you cooperate, you will all walk out of here perfectly fine. If you choose not to cooperate, then you will end up like that gentleman you see laying over there covered in blood next to Vito," said Cat.

They all looked over at the body. Lydia began to cry out loud.

"Now here is the deal: First of all, I need you to shut the fuck up. Next thing you need to know is, this is a robbery, not any kind of robbery, but a jux. Yes, you heard me correctly.

It's a jux. You all have large sums of money, and my friends and I want some of it. Now if you're nice and give us what we want, then like I said, you will not be harmed. This is how it will go. Each of you will give us the location where you keep your cash stashed and the layout of your place and how to get to it. Two of us will leave here to retrieve the money. If all checks out, then we will call our friend and let him know that you were right on the money. If the information that you give is false, then that call to our friend will be to kill you. You will be killed in cold blood, as an example to whoever is next. If by some chance we are not able to call our friend due to some untold information, such as running into an alarm system that would alert the cops, or a security guard that might land us into the hands of the cops, then all of you will be killed by our friend."

When Cat was done talking, he slowly looked at all of them. "I hope I made myself clear!"

One by one, with a pen and a pad in hand, Cat questioned each of the victims. He started off with Vito. He took the duct tape from his mouth, and Vito began talking immediately about his safe, giving the location and combination. When he was done, Cat placed the tape back on his mouth and moved on to the next person.

CAT AND HIS MEN EXITED the party using one of the catering vans. Cat drove not a mile over or under the speed limit. He left the highway onto South Ocean Boulevard. All the homes in South Ocean were multimillion-dollar estates. He drove for about seven minutes, slowing down just enough to see the addresses on each house.

"This should be it right here," said James, looking through the window to check the address. "Yeah, this is it."

The van turned into the driveway and stopped. Cat reached outside the window with the security card Vito had given him and swiped it into the box. Slowly the gate on the sprawling house began to open. Once they drove through, it closed behind them. They drove up the driveway past the palm trees, Greek statues, and huge water fountains. It was a two-minute drive from the front gates to the house. They pulled up at the front door. They did not need to sneak around because they had the keys to the house and its entire layout. The two of them got out of the van, and with the same security card, Cat swiped the door and it opened. James's eyes widened as Cat pushed the door open to reveal the inside of the house. Nothing but opulence.

Perfection to satisfy the most discriminating taste.

"This is what the fuck I'm talking about here. This is the type of shit motherfucker should be owning and living in," exclaimed James, as he briefly fantasized that he and Symone lived here.

The house was a ten-bedroom palace. It featured two huge master suites, four terraces, two pools, a steam room, exercise gym, four Jacuzzis, and thirteen wide-screen televisions, two of which were in a theater. There were also swim-up bars in the pools and a mini golf course. It's total worth was $26 million.

THE PARTY WAS STILL IN full swing. The music was blasting and the DJ was rocking the house. It took an hour and a half to refill the pool. People were losing their clothes to jump in.

Inside the garage, Gamble was dressed up in a tux and masked like the rest of the team. Pacing back and forth in the garage, he had a gun at his waist, playing the intimidation game with everybody.

James, Cat, and Prince were now on their fourth house. They had already successfully completed robbing Vito, Lydia, and a third house as well. After each one, they placed a call to Gamble and let him know that all was good and well. Traces of smiles were on Lydia's and Vito's faces after the call came in for the fourth robbery. They were getting closer to getting out of a crazy situation.

Suddenly, the bloody man lying next to Vito began to move. Everyone in the room noticed it as they looked at him in horror.

"I can see by the look on your face that you are wondering what you are doing here all tied up and covered in blood. Not to worry, me friend, you will be fine providing that these kind people have given my friends the right information that we need to rob them of their money. Oh, and don't worry, that's only chicken blood that you're covered in. You were used as a scare tactic to convince them that we are serious and we mean business," Gamble said to the man covered in blood.

"WAIT A MINUTE, I GOT it, I fucking got it! I know how we could get into that damn party and crash it without violating any rules or laws," said Hemming.

"Well, if you have something, spill it already. The rest of us are waiting to hear this great idea," yelled Tina.

"We could go in with the fire marshal."

"What?" asked Timothy.

"Look, if we could get it okayed by the captain to call the fire marshal, explain to them our situation and what we need, I'm sure that they would be willing to show up here under the pretense of an inspection to see if the party was violating any fire codes, such as overcrowding. We would be able to slip right in with them. Once we identify who we are looking for, we could start shutting the party down and grabbing all of the evidence."

"Man, that is a brilliant fucking idea! Damn, why the hell didn't you come up with it sooner? I'll call the captain and run this one by him. It just might work," said Timothy excitedly as he picked up the phone in the truck.

IT WAS THREE O'CLOCK IN the afternoon and many of the partygoers had gone home to bathe and freshen up before returning and continuing to party. The crew had finished transferring the money from the catering truck to the green van that they had stolen. It was time to make their exit. The four of them got into the van with Gamble as the driver, since technically he was not wanted like the rest of them. Even though they all had new IDs, they did not want to run the risk with all that money that they were carrying.

The garage door opened and the van drove out, the door quickly closing behind them. They drove down the driveway and up to the gate. Gamble stuck his head out for the security guard to see him. The guard pressed the release button and the gate began to open. As they got about two blocks away, they saw and heard the fire engines race toward them. They pulled over to the side and allowed them to pass. Four unmarked cars were following the fire engines.

"I wonder where they're going?" asked Prince, laughing.

After the cars passed, the van continued on its way. The fire trucks raced to a stop at the front gate, where the chief jumped out and told the security men that they would be arrested if they tried to impede entry into the house. The big man stepped aside and opened the gate, then got on his radio and gave the heads-up that the firemen along with the cops were coming in.

Bull quickly began to dispose of the drugs in crock pots filled with hot oil. The cocaine and ecstasy quickly dissolved in the oil. The pots were on wheels, so as the oil dissolved the drugs, Bull and a lady friend dragged the two huge pots into the bathroom, where they began pouring the oil and liquefied drugs into the toilet. Then they simply flushed them away.

Another female friend of Bull's ran into the powder room. The three of them hurried upstairs to the master bedroom, where Bull began to tape the money to their bodies.

"It must be in another room," said Hemming.

The task force began searching throughout the house, checking the other rooms. By this time Bull was done wrapping the money onto the females' bodies, and they walked out into the hallway blending in with everyone else.

The girls made their way through the house and outside through the throngs of people, then they filed out the front gate.

The task force quickly moved in to detain Bull. He was all they had. They took Bull from the party, put him in a car, and drove him down to headquarters to interrogate him.

On the final day of the party, things were still live without Gamble. Back at the storage yard, the money machine was counting its final stack of cash. When it was done, it was rubber-banded up and placed into bags. A total of $305 million was split up equally among them. With their money bagged up, and ready to make their final exit, they decided to have a toast. Cat pulled out a bottle of VSOP and some plastic cups. He handed out the cups, then opened the bottle and began to pour them the liquor. Cat, Prince, and James poured some out to the ground for Ozzi.

"Wish you was here, my nigga," said Prince.

"Word up," said James.

"Man, I can't believe it, I would have never guessed it in a million years about Cloud," said Prince.

"Word, I can't believe that shit either!" said James.

"It's all adding up now," Prince said. "I'll never forget that jux he fucked up. He kinda hesitated a bit when we had to dust the bitch."

"That's why nobody couldn't find him when it was time to split up. We came really close to letting this motherfucker take us down," said James.

"That bottom boy killed Ozzi and lock up Banit! I'm for dead star!"

"For real, me get him head lick off!"

"Here's to Banit," said Cat, holding up his cup of liquor.

"To Banit!" Prince said.

"That nigga gave the ultimate sacrifice. He was running around looking for you," Cat said, referring to James. "He let us know what was up with that Cloud when he was free and could've gotten away. He made all of this possible."

"Much love to Banit." Prince poured a little of his liquor out of his cup.

Cat did the same, then held his cup up. "And to the jux!"

"To the jux!" they repeated.

"Respect it," said Cat.

"It's respected," replied James and Prince. Gamble followed and repeated after them.

After they drank, it was time to split up. With their money and new identification provided to them by Cynthia, they walked out of the storage yard, leaving the van behind. The four of them said their good-byes and were off in four separate cars that they had stolen and parked out back. They headed toward I-95 North in the direction of Orlando.

Cat stopped off in Orange County, where he boxed up his money and mailed it off to Carroll. James and Prince continued north. Prince stopped off in Atlanta at his mother's house, where he gave her instructions to send his money to him in Jamaica. James continued on to New York with plans of launching his record company, a business in which he could wash his money. He also couldn't wait to put his arms around Symone, who would be thrilled to no end when she saw his haul. Cynthia headed to Orlando to catch her flight to Los Angeles, where she was to meet Cat. Cynthia and Cat had made plans to flee the country once the last jux was done. From California they would fly together to Mexico, then to Trinidad. England would be their final place of residence.

GAMBLE WAS SCHEDULED FOR A cruise leaving Orlando to the Bahamas. From there, he planned to fly to Brazil, where he would buy his yacht and set out on his voyage of the sea.

Gamble placed his bags on the trolley to be taken onto the ship. As he moved up in line, he saw police and the ship's security running toward the line of people. His heart almost jumped through his mouth. He nervously held his head down trying to hide his face as they got closer. His legs were saying run. He tried desperately to hold on to his composure. Fortunately, the police ran right past him and onto the ship. Then he saw two paramedics running behind the police. The line stopped moving. About twenty minutes later the paramedics and the police along with the ship's security brought a man off the ship on a gurney, an IV hooked up to him.

Gamble closed his eyes and let out a deep sigh of relief.

EPILOGUE

Cat and Cynthia married and lived well in England. They traveled all over Europe, from France to Italy to Germany and Russia. The following year, they planned to travel all over Africa and visit all the historic sights as they did in Europe.

On a beautiful moonlit night, at about eleven o'clock, Cat and Cynthia had just finished eating at a restaurant. As they walked into the parking lot to their car, they were approached by two young men between the ages of seventeen and twenty.

"Hey, mister, you have a light?"

"Sorry, but I don't smoke," Cat replied.

Suddenly the other man brandished a gun. "Well, you gonna be smoked if you don't hand over your jewelry and wallet! You, too, miss!"

The boy with the gun was closest to Cat. The gun was pointed only five inches from Cat's stomach. Cat looked down at the gun, then looked in the young man's eyes, seeing that he was not even paying attention to Cat. He was busy watching his friend relieving Cynthia of her jewelry. Cat realized that he could, with his military training, easily disarm the young man and take him down, but he decided not to as he looked at the both of them and smiled.

Respect the jux!

FIVE STICKUPS

(based on actual events)

STICKUP 1

In 1990, Prince had just returned home after a two-year bid. His nephew Dadz, who was his stickup partner, was in duckdown mode after putting two hot ones in a nigga.

The older of the two, Prince began his crime wave in the late seventies, while Dadz joined his uncle in 1984. Although they grew up separately, the two were close. They always wanted to work together on some get-money shit, so they started doing stickups. Their family loyalty made them a deadly combination. No matter how many bullets were sent flying or how dangerous the situation, they covered each other's back. Each knew the other would not leave him even if it would cost him his own life.

After coming home from jail, Prince needed

money. Being on the run and unable to get his hustle fully on, Dadz, too, was in need of some cash. Now was the perfect time. They planned a jux on Lenny, a pimp out in Queensbridge. He was one of the old-timers and had been pimping since the late sixties.

One of Prince's boys was also a pimp and didn't like Lenny, so he gave Prince the rundown on Lenny. Once Prince hollered at Dadz about this jux, it was on.

At about midnight, Dadz and Prince pulled up and parked down the block from the ho strip. Dadz had borrowed his girl's car for the jux. They parked where they were able to see the entire strip. They watched all the pimps and hos doing their business all night.

They spotted Lenny from the jump and kept their eyes on him. Lenny had a custom-made van that he used to transport his hos. He also sat in it watching his hos on the strip to make sure that they were getting that paper right. Lenny's van was parked down the other end of the ho stroll. Occasionally, he would get out of the van to have a word with his prostitutes and collect whatever money they had on them.

Prince and Dadz watched the strip until about 5 a.m., just as the sun was coming up, and when they were sure Lenny had brought in enough money to make the jux worthwhile.

The pimps were beginning to leave the strip. This was the moment the two had been waiting for. Old-time pimps kinda looked out for each other, and they didn't want Lenny to have any help.

Prince and Dadz exited the car and walked around the block. The plan was to come up on the side block as if they were customers (tricks). When they came around the block, making their way down a side street, they saw one of the pimps on the strip coming in their direction with his three hos. Just as the pimp nigga got to them, Dadz popped off his tool and grabbed ahold of him. Without hesitation, Prince went into action as he popped off his tool and jux down the three hos as well. Dadz went through the pimp's pockets and took all his money off him. Prince lined the hos up next to the pimp. The hos were calm as if they had been through this before.

"Listen, and listen good! Just be cool and everything gonna be all right, ya dig?" asked Dadz.

"Yeah, man, I got ya," replied the pimp.

"That's good, so what's your name?"

"Roger."

"Dis da deal. You ain't the one we want. Who we want is Lenny, but I'ma need your help. I need you to walk us down to his van so we don't look suspicious approaching it. You got that?" Dadz spoke in a calm but sarcastic tone.

"Yeah, nigga, aight."

They all began to walk down the block toward Lenny's van. As they walked, Dadz instructed Roger on what to do and not do.

"When you get to the van, I want you to tell him that you got some tricks who want about six girls, so that motherfucker opens the door. Don't try no funny shit unless you want a hole in your fucking head."

As they reached the door of the van, Roger called out, "Yo, Lenny."

Lenny rolled his window down. Prince was standing behind one of the hos while Dadz went around the other side of the van. Lenny was getting ready to call it quits for the night so his four hos and his bodyguard were in the van. The bodyguard was in the passenger seat, so when Roger got to Lenny's door and called to him, the bodyguard also looked in that direction. Because of that, he didn't see Dadz when he came around to his side.

"What's up, Rog?" asked Lenny as he leaned through the window.

"I got a couple of tricks here who want some extra hos."

"Oh yeah? Aight that sounds good."

Lenny began to open his door. Just as he

pulled the lock up, Prince grabbed the handle, opened the door, then threw his gun into Lenny's face.

"Move over, pussy bouy!"

The bodyguard realized it was a jux and tried to slide out through the other door. As he began to slide out, he felt steel in the back of his neck.

"Where the fuck you think you're going? Get the fuck back in there!"

Prince and Dadz put Roger and his three girls into the van as well. After everyone was inside, the two stripped them of their jewelry and money. The bodyguard decided to do his job and test them, but he picked the wrong stickup team to be brave on. Prince, the more aggressive of the two, let loose on him, beating him to a pulp while Dadz sat back watching with a smirk of delight.

"Which one of you made the most money for the night?" Dadz asked the hos.

One of them raised her hand.

"Take your draws off!" he ordered her.

She did as she was told.

"You wanna be a bodyguard? Well, who is gonna guard you, Mr. Bodyguard?" asked Prince. "Come over here!" he told the prostitute. "I want you to sit on his face and rub your pussy in his mouth. You got that? Rub your nasty pussy all over his face."

"Yes."

Prince put his gun to the bodyguard's neck and told him to open his mouth. Prince and Dadz laughed as the ho rubbed her pussy in his mouth. The two came up with a nice little $7,000 for the night.

STICKUP 2

SUMMER OF 1990, BROKE AND with no money in his pocket, not even for gas, Prince decided this would be a perfect time to jux Tens, a weed dealer with several weed spots in Jamaica, Queens. Prince knew him well because before he moved out to Jamaica, his old hustling grounds were in Corona.

Although Prince was never able to get his hands on Tens himself, he'd juxed several of his spots so many times that the crew knew him now. You would think that after a couple of times getting robbed, they would put a gun in the store, but the spots were well-known by the police and Tens risked serious gun charges should the spot get raided. Getting busted for weed was not as serious as gun possession.

Tens did not know Dadz, so Prince instructed him on what to do. Dadz did not really like to run up in places because of the many blind spots. He knew a couple of stickup kids who caught bad ones like this. But with no money, he said fuck it.

They parked around the corner from Parsons Boulevard, got out, and walked. Prince fell behind as Dadz went ahead to the door. The worker in the spot looked at Dadz, then buzzed the door to let him in. Once the door opened, he walked in slowly. Prince was a second too late and the door closed on him. The worker looked at Prince and smiled at his not being able to get in.

"Buzz that shit, motherfucker!" said Dadz.

The worker turned around to see this big Taurus nozzle pointing in his face. He quickly and nervously buzzed the door. Pushing it open, Prince had a cigarette in his mouth. As he walked in, he took the cigarette from his mouth and threw it at the worker. It hit him dead in his eye.

"What the fuck was you smiling about? Like you wasn't trying to let me up in here to get this money, motherfucker?" Prince snatched the worker from behind the counter and dragged him to the back, where he began stomping him out. "Don't ever try to protect someone else's money like it's yours, nigga. You just a fucking worker, so whenever you see me coming, you buzz that fucking door. You got that, you bitch!"

Prince and Dadz bagged up the weed and money and began to make their exit. They did not have anything to tie the worker up with, so they just left him in the back. As they walked out of the store, a police car was driving by. It stopped at a red light, only a few feet from the store. The robbers walked in the opposite direction. As they got about a half block away, the worker ran out toward the police car and told them that the store was just robbed and the robbers were heading down the block now. Prince and Dadz looked back and saw the police car reverse, so they took off running around the corner to their car. They made it into the car just in time.

STICKUP 3

A WEEK LATER PRINCE AND Dadz were broke again. Since the last spot they juxed went off without a hitch, Dadz decided that they would try another one. This time he decided to do a candy store in Flushing, Queens, owned by another dread.

Again they parked around the block and walked around the corner and into the store. They popped their guns off as soon as they got into the store and ordered the dread to open the door that led behind the counter. The dread was barricaded behind a bulletproof glass panel. He put his big chrome .357 up on the counter.

"If you know what I know, the two of you would walk out of here the same way you came in here now," said the dread.

Dadz and Prince left. A half hour later, Prince and Dadz walked back into the store with two milk bottles filled with gasoline. They sprinkled the liquid all over the store, on the bulletproof glass, and into the serving slot. When they were done, they stood by the door.

"All right, dread, how you want to do this? You can either burn the fuck up in here or you can start passing the weed and money and that gun through the slot there. You've got until I count to ten." Prince pulled on his cigarette, making the tip glow. When he got to seven, the dread opened the slot and began to pass out the drugs, money, and gun.

STICKUP 4

One of Dadz's homeys that he grew up was hustling outta state. He knew that Dadz was in duckdown mode and in need of some cash. He decided to let him get at his connect since he was about to stop fucking with him for another connect with better prices.

Dadz's man started to take him uptown with him whenever he went to cop so the connect would get used to his face and wouldn't act strange when Dadz came without him. His man would give Dadz some of the money that he would be using to re-up with, to make it look as though Dadz was copping his own work.

"All he gotta do is take me up there with him to cop one more time and we good. I should be able to go up there by myself and cop from them, then, bong, we got them," Dadz said to Prince.

"So when is the next time y'all going up there?"

"As a matter of fact, we going tonight."

"So by when you think we could get at them?" asked Prince.

"I would say by Friday."

"Why so long?"

"Friday is good, this way it don't look suspicious. Plus you know Friday is usually a busy day anyway. By the time we get at them, they should have a nice cash stash built up. We want the cash more than the drugs."

"Fuck it. I'm wit it, whatever!"

It was Friday. Dadz and his man had already made the last buy from their connect. They were some Dominicans who were moving weight in Harlem. However, this set of Dominicans weren't as vigilant when it came to security as most of them were that dealt in weight. Dadz and Prince turned off Douglass and onto 144th Street, where the building was located. They only wanted to drive by first to get a look at the block. A few dudes were standing outside, plus the lookout that usually took the customers upstairs to where they would do business. They drove ahead to Powell Boulevard and made a right turn. They were now looking for somewhere to park. As they drove slowly, Prince spotted a car pulling out of a parking spot.

"Yo, right there, right there, pull up quick," Prince said, pointing at the spot.

Dadz pulled up and began to parallel park. Halfway into the spot, Dadz said, "Hold up."

"What's up?"

"I don't think that we should get all jammed up in this parking spot like this."

"Why, what's up?"

"Suppose something pops off and we need to make a quick break. It's gonna be too much time wasted trying to get outta this parking space."

"Yeah, you right on that," Prince said as he thought about it. "I'm saying though, we gotta park somewhere."

Dadz rubbed on his chin for a second while he thought about it. "Fuck it, I think we should just double-park right here."

"Man, this is Harlem, you gonna get a ticket before you even walk around the corner."

"I'd rather deal with a ticket than getting caught up in a worse situation. At least a nigga could pay his way out of a ticket. But a nigga ain't paying his way outta no bullets!"

"That's real shit there. Fuck it then, the ticket it is."

They pulled out of the spot and double-parked. They then checked their guns to make sure they were on point and ready for use. Dadz had a MP5, with its eighty-clip magazine; it was easy to tell that he wasn't taking any chances running up in the Dominican spot. Prince was handling a MAC-11. Though it didn't take as many bullets, with its thirty-round clip, it was clear that he came prepared as well.

They walked up to the building entrance, where Dadz spotted the lookout in front. He and Prince walked up to him.

"Hey, my man, what's up?" the lookout said to Dadz as they gave each other five and a hood hug.

"Nothing much, my friend, just here to do some business."

"Okay, that's good. Where's your friend, Dee?"

"Oh, he still outta town. He should be here tomorrow."

"Okay, that's good."

"I brought my man with me, too."

The lookout looked over Dadz's shoulder at Prince. "That's good, really good, my friend."

They then turned and walked past the rest of the guys that were standing outside. The apartment where the deals went down was on the third floor. They took the stairs instead of the elevator. They came to the apartment door and stopped. The lookout knocked on the door six times. Recognizing the code, a fella with gel-spiked hair opened the door without looking through the peephole or asking who it was. He recognized Dadz. The lookout said something in Spanish, and the spike-haired man began to smile.

"Come in," he said in badly broken English.

He opened the door wider to let them in. The three of them walked in, and when they got to the living room, another man came out from the back room down the hall. The spiked-hair fella said something to him in Spanish, then motioned to Dadz and Prince to come with him.

This was the typical routine. Dadz was up on this. The deals usually went down in the back room. The other two men waited out in the front room. Prince and Dadz entered the back room and were now out of sight from the two men in the front.

"*Siéntense,*" the dealer said, pointing at the chairs by the table in the middle of the room.

The dealer turned his back to the robbers as he walked over to a box that was sitting in the corner. Dadz and Prince pulled out their guns and handcuffs. Dadz doubled back to the living room to handle the two out front. When the dealer turned around, Prince had his gun right on his lip.

"Shhhh. Not a fucking sound, motherfucker!" he said in a whisper.

Dadz came around the corner. The other two were facing each other talking.

"Put your hands up, put your fucking hands up!" The two men froze. "Oh, you acting like you don't understand me, mother—I said put your fucking hands up!" Dadz poked the lookout in the mouth really hard with the muzzle of the gun, busting his lip.

The lookout men put their hands up in the air. Dadz handed them a set of handcuffs.

"Cuff yourself to each other," Dadz ordered.

They did as they were told. Dadz handed them another set of handcuffs and told them to cuff themselves to the radiator. Both were secured. Dadz walked over and began to search them. He took the jewelry and pocket money they had on them.

"Yo, what up?" Prince called out.

"I'm good out here."

Prince had cuffed up the other one in the room to the radiator. They put the cocaine and the money that they found in the box and put it into a bag. To make their exit, they tucked away their guns, then opened the door and looked out into the hallway. Dadz walked out first. Prince held on to the bag. They walked down the steps and out the building, past the dudes that were standing outside. Halfway up the block, they heard someone shout out something in Spanish. They knew from the urgency in the voice that their deed had been discovered. Prince was several yards in front of Dadz since he had the bag with the money and drugs, and Dadz had his weapon. The men from in front of the building were advancing toward them and reached for their guns. It was about to go down. Dadz saw the first gun come out.

"Go ahead, get to the car!" he screamed as he threw Prince the car keys.

Walking backward, Dadz pulled out the MP5 and clicked the safety off. Prince started to run. Dadz did not wait; he aimed the MP5 and opened it up. Shots were coming back, but with the ferocity of the MP5, the Dominicans scattered for cover. Prince jumped in the car and started it. Dadz was right on his tail.

STICKUP 5

NITTY, FIFTEEN YEARS OLD, AND Boogie, seventeen years old, were best friends since the fifth grade. They lived in the East New York section of Brooklyn, two teenage boys who took to the streets after their hardworking mothers were unable to keep an eye on them. They started off selling packs (crack packages) for an older hustler in the hood. Their cut was forty/sixty—40 percent their way, 60 percent to their boss. The money was enough for the youngsters to buy their little sneakers and fly gear. But they couldn't take the long hours required out on the block, especially in weather five degrees below freezing.

One night, the two boys witnessed a robbery by one of the older guys in the hood. They saw how quick and easy it was to come up with fast cash. They tried their hand at this new way of getting money. They started off strong-arming the younger kids in the neighborhood, who were afraid of them.

Shortly thereafter they started stickups when Nitty got his hands on a .25-caliber handgun for $50. With a gun, they could move on to something bigger. They set their eyes on a numbers spot in their neighborhood, owned and operated by some old-time Colombian.

They scoped out the joint. They took notice of one of the men who would always leave the store with a bag near closing time. He must have been carrying the money that was collected for the day. They focused on him. Every night they followed him to learn his daily routine.

They discovered that he would walk down Flushing Avenue and make a right on Graham Avenue, where he would get into a waiting car. The plan was to get at him before he got to the car. They could not do it on Flushing Avenue because it was too busy. They decided to make their move as soon as the Colombian made the turn onto Graham Avenue.

It was Saturday night. The weather was about thirty-five degrees with a steady wind blowing. The two decided to go ahead to the spot on Graham where they would make their move. They were leaning on a car, pretending to be minding their own business, as the man rounded the corner. As he approached, Nitty had his hands in his pockets. His right hand was on the gun in his coat pocket. When the man got directly in front of them, Nitty pulled out the gun and put it in the man's face without saying a word. Boogie went straight for the bag, grabbing hold of it and attempting to pull it free from the man's grip, to no avail. The man did not let go of his bag.

"Get off the fucking bag, old man," yelled Boogie as he struggled for the bag.

Nitty grabbed hold of the man's shirt and pointed the gun at his chest. "Get off!" he barked.

The man refused to let go of the bag.

Bang!

The old-timer's grasp loosened as he stumbled back holding his chest. The old-timer did not hit the ground. He caught his balance and began to scream for help.

Nitty and Boogie both took off running down the block past the waiting car. They rounded the corner at Humboldt and Graham and kept on running until they reached Nitty's building. They ran up the steps to the top floor. They were out of breath. Boogie reached down and unzipped the bag. They could not believe their eyes.

"What the fuck is that?" asked Nitty.

Boogie reached into the bag and began to move the papers to the side hoping to find some cash underneath, but as he dug down, all he found were more papers. The bag was filled with nothing but numbers papers.

The above events are true. However, the details have been altered slightly to protect those who were involved.

POCKET READERS GROUP GUIDE

RESPECT THE

FRANK C. MATTHEWS

INTRODUCTION

As a kid growing up in Jamaica, Cat learned that life was simple: you hustle, or you get hustled. He decided that he wanted to get his, and he wasn't going to let the law stop him. Then at sixteen, his world was uprooted and brought to the streets of Queens. Cat's first jux happened after spotting a "baller," a man with a knot of cash. He was too flashy with his cash, so it was taken from him. This is the code Cat lives by; this is the code that gives rise to The Order of Thieves.

The Order, founded by Cat, consists of a disparate group of men who have all proved themselves in action. They do not consider themselves gangsters, but gunmen; they go down shooting. Cat, Banit, Cloud, James, Prince, and Ozzi are the members, but one of them is a cop, and one of them is about to get killed. Forced to split up, the crew plans to reunite in Miami and team with party promoter Gamble to pull off the biggest jux any of them has ever seen. Will their pasts catch up with them before they can pull it off, or will they be able to leave the streets with a newly stolen fortune?

QUESTIONS FOR DISCUSSION

1. The fascinating account of Cat's rise is told in Chapter Two. Arriving in the United States at sixteen, he had already lived the life of a thug in Jamaica, and his father was murdered in gang activity when Cat was just a boy. Do you think Cat had a way out of life on the streets, or was it inevitable? Given his story, does any part of you admire the success he achieved in founding The Order?

2. Cat's first jux is committed after he sees a man he calls "the baller," with gold chains and gold rings, pull out a knot of thousands of dollars and take out a few bills for groceries. This conspicuous display of wealth makes Cat both angry and jealous. Throughout the novel Cat and The Order prey on people who flaunt their wealth, as if the victims are receiving their comeuppance for being so flashy. What do you think of this system of justice? How much of a jux do you think is the victim's fault?

3. We witness Cloud's trepidation in the middle of a jux at the onset of the novel, and soon learn that he is a cop. Given this revelation, what do you think of his participa-

tion and the shot he fires in the opening jux? Should he be punished by the law? Also, do you think he intentionally didn't search the man thoroughly, hoping that a member of The Order would be shot, or do you believe it was just an oversight?

4. Even though Banit "felt responsible for Ozzi's death," should he have gone to Ozzi's funeral or was that foolish? Why do you think none of the other members of The Order went?

5. One of the most interesting relationships in the novel was between Prince and his nephew James. What did you make of this family tag-team? Was it irresponsible of Prince to encourage this behavior in James, or was he simply looking out for a man who was going to be a criminal anyway, and keeping him close?

6. In Chapters Five and Six, we get a glimpse of what a loose cannon James is, as he murders first Allen and then Vill. We then see rogue justice played out again as James is gunned down in Chapter Seven. Do you think the members of The Order would agree that James deserved this judging by

the rules of their own code? Do you think he got what he deserved?

7. Banit's initiation into The Order is one of the most poignant and intimate scenes in the novel. It reveals a sensitive side to Cat, and gives us glimpses into his reasons for founding it. During the oath, Banit must repeat, "I . . . swear with my life to uphold The Order. To obey and follow all its rules and to always strive to better the principles it is founded upon and to walk in their deeper meanings." Discuss this initiation and the rituals that Cat lays out. What do you think these deeper meanings are? Do you think all of the members of The Order fully understand?

8. The reasons for Gamble's assimilation into the crew were simple; he knew everyone in Miami, he helped Cat and The Order gain access to some of the most important people around, and he also helped plan the super jux at the end of the novel. He never officially became a member of The Order, but do you think he will? Will The Order continue as we know it, or do you think it is over with?

9. Judging by Cloud and Tina's failure to get into the party and stop the super jux, The Order

definitely prevailed. But did the good guys win, or did the bad guys win? Think about the case of Cloud. Was justice thwarted, or did it win out? Do you like Cloud for being on the side of the law, or hate Cloud for being crooked?

10. In retrospect, which of the juxes performed in the novel was your favorite, and why? Some likely candidates include Cat's initial solo jux on "the baller," the jux on the Chinese man, the jux that the novel begins with, and the super jux at the end. What do you think?

11. What do you make of the five real juxes included at the end of the book, referred to as Five Stickups? Do they help to bring you some perspective on the rest of the novel, or stand alone as an interesting footnote?

12. The novel ends with a very interesting message: Everything is cyclical. After Cat and Cynthia have traveled the world, and are living the life, they fall victim to a jux. Cat could have stopped it, but deemed it more important to "respect the jux." It got him where he is, so why stop others from getting there too? Do you think Cat will ever commit another jux, or is he officially retired? Would Cat be a hypocrite if he broke up the jux?

ENHANCE YOUR BOOK CLUB

1. Take the imaginative leap and assume this will become a movie. If you were to cast the main characters, which actors/actresses would you chose to play the role of Cat? Cloud? Prince and James? Ozzi? Banit? Gamble? Cynthia? Create your own cast list, chose a director, then compare notes with your fellow book club members and see how many names you have in common.

2. Check out the author Facebook page for *Respect the Jux* at www.facebook.com/frankcmatthews or his website at http://keeplockent.com. You can see updates from the author, order T-shirts with the cover art, and revisit everything that you loved about the novel.

3. You have just read about several juxes in the novel and seen five other examples of juxes that actually occurred, so with your newly learned expertise diagram the next jux for Cat and The Order. Will it be overseas in London or somewhere new in the U.S.? Which members of The Order will be there? Will Gamble be involved? Either create a scenario individually or have your reading group agree upon one.

AUTHOR QUESTIONS

Q: Like Cat, you started hustling and became a man of the streets at a young age. How autobiographical was this novel, and was it difficult to keep yourself from transposing your own experiences onto your character?

A: It is not autobiographical, however, I have witnessed all that I write about in some form, shape, or fashion. There are only two degrees of separation between what I write and what I live.

Q: Did you ever consider writing the book as a piece of nonfiction? How do you think your audience would react to the story if the specifics of the juxes were presented as facts?

A: No, I am unable to write it as a piece of nonfiction without incriminating others. I think they would react the same because the jux is something that occurs every day. There's someone being juxed at this very moment.

Q: How did being incarcerated change the way you approach telling a story like this? Is it easier to let your imagination wander? More difficult to conjure up images? Do you think you ever would have written the story if you were not incarcerated?

A: Being incarcerated added a little depth to my story-telling ability, but overall I do think I would have written a story of this magnitude. This story comes from my element and era so it's not hard to let my mind wander or conjure up images, it's a natural flow—similar to a hip-hop artist writing a song.

Q: You mention that, while serving time, you read everything you could get your hands on. Were there any specific writers that influenced your style and subject matter? Who would you want to be compared to as a writer?

A: I would not want to be compared to anybody because I wouldn't want to credit or discredit any other author. I'm just Frank C. Matthews telling Frank C. Matthews stories.

Q: Do you think the fact that you have lived some of the situations in the book gives you instant credibility with your readers, or do you still feel like you need to earn their respect?

A: The fact that I lived some of these situations naturally gives me credibility, however, I do feel a need to earn the respect of my readers because all of my books are not about criminal experiences. I'm a well-rounded person, I attended college and made decent grades when I was at school, as well as traveled the world. I want everyone to both understand and appreciate my work.

Q: The book is hard to categorize because it is so real and raw, and it doesn't seem right to give it a blanket classification. What genre would you place yourself in? Urban Fiction? Crime Fiction?

A: I categorize my genre as "True Fiction." There is truth to every story I write and there's a Cat out there whose life reflects my writing.

Q: At the conclusion of the book you include five "Stickups" which recount juxes that actually occurred. Why did you decide to include these five historical juxes?

A: I wanted to give my readers more. I wanted them to feel how authentic my writing is, and the essence of my stories.

Q: You have written a total of twenty books while doing time, though this is the first one that is being published. What advice would you give to aspiring writers who want to break into the business? How many of your works did you send out to publishers before you signed your book deal?

A: I would tell any writer who wants to break into the business to offer something different to his or her readers. Work harder than anyone who's working with you or for you. Maintain a positive attitude and never take no for an answer. I only sent one of my books,

Respect the Jux, out to publishers. However, it took me five years to get a publishing deal. So you can never give up on your dream.

Q: Do you have any plans to reunite Cat, James, Banit, and the rest of The Order for any future novels, or do you prefer to work with different characters on different projects?

A: I will reunite The Order, so stay tuned for Part Two. I will also be introducing other characters to the world in other books such as *Bury Me in It*, *Below the Radar*, *Through My Dog's Eyes*, *Summer of the Dons*, and *Lucifer Godson*, to name a few.